Driven

NEW HEIGHTS PUBLISHING
www.suzannefalter.com

Book cover design by Caroline Manchoulis
www.ladylit.com

Book design by Danielle H. Acee
www.authorsassistant.com

ISBN: 978-0-9969981-3-0

Driven

An Oaktown Girls Novel

a novel by
SUZANNE **FALTER**

Many thanks to the following folks who made the writing of this book possible:

My awesome production team, Danielle Hartman Acee and Danylle Salinas of The Authors' Assistant. Cover artist, Caroline Manchoulis. Jack Harvey, who got behind this project. And thanks as ever to my spouse, for her thoughtful edits and her huge support.

I'd also like to thank the women of Oakland who gathered around me to offer friendship and enthusiasm for this project. You know who you are.

Chapter One

Tenika Cummins lifted the door to the garage with a heave, and listened to it loudly clatter up into its housing. She opened the place with the same orchestrated sequence of steps every morning. Open door. Start coffeemaker. Check messages. Survey the terrain. She never tired of its beautiful familiarity, even after nearly a decade.

But this morning, Tenika added another step. Digging into the worn leather satchel she wore over her shoulder, she dug out a perfectly hollowed out half-pineapple with a white pillar candle nested inside of it. She walked over to the small altar in the corner, put it down in a place of prominence, pulled out a lighter and lit it. This was her offering to Ogun, the Yoruba god of iron, known for clearing obstacles to prosperity among other things. *Ogun, please do your thing*, she pleaded silently.

Because, basically, someone had to get this train moving again.

Tenika was a tall, fast-moving woman with a calm efficiency about her. For this reason, her friends called her "The Fixer." She was usually a blur of dreadlocks and glasses once she got going. And she was always the first person they turned to when they dropped their smart phones in the toilet or locked their keys in their car. Tenika knew how to fix pretty much anything, especially cars. It had never been totally clear how or why she had such developed mechanical skills, but her reputation was well-established among the

East Bay lesbians. As for Tenika, she just assumed she was some sort of natural-born "life engineer." She could *feel* how to fix things… and so she did.

Tenika hummed as she moved along, feeling inspired by her offering to Ogun. This was going to work. She just knew it. Something had to, that was for damn sure. Their appointment book had been close to empty for the last two weeks, and she just couldn't take one more day of her business partner moping around like she was near death or something. It was only a business, for Lord's sake, even if it *was* theirs.

Tenika placed a filter in the aging, stained basket of the Mr. Coffee and measured out five scoops of Bustelo. Then she carried the glass coffee pot over to the tap and filled it. Everything around her had a slight layer of grime. It was an ever-present dinginess that neither she nor Lizzy saw much anymore. But she saw it now.

Boy, did she see it.

This was all because of the walk Tenika had taken through downtown Oakland the night before. It was getting on to 10:00 p.m. when she and her partner, Delilah, stopped to peer into the windows of the recently opened garage, and there was the evidence right in front of them.

Six shiny, new massage chairs were lined up in front of the window. Behind them, a space barely recognizable as a garage sported gleaming painted concrete floors, impeccable lifts, and, yes, even a sushi bar off to the side. It looked more like a dealership than a garage. Or, hell, even some high-end boutique hotel lobby. There wasn't even a single greasy tool lying around. In fact, there wasn't a tool in sight at all. Tenika wondered where they kept them.

Above them, the sign said it all:

Mindy Rose's All-Star Garage and Sushi Bar
The Garage with Class

Well, what did one expect from a garage that opened up in the space formerly occupied by Whole Foods? Or from an owner who was a former professional race car driver with fake tits, and was busy reinventing herself?

Mindy fucking Rose, Tenika thought with dismay.

Shit.

She stood holding the dripping coffee pot for a moment, considering her surroundings. Her eye went to the sign at their own entrance that said 'Driven Garage—Woman-Owned, Woman-Powered.' That used to be all it took to get the loyal lesbians to show up in droves. But now, well, no one seemed to care anymore if any damn thing was woman-owned. Being a lesbian was downright commonplace. Quaint, even, in this age of gender fluidity.

Tenika pushed her glasses back on her nose and set her jaw.

Was it possible that all the lesbians had deserted them for sushi and a chair massage? Tenika did her best to ignore the surge of fear that passed through her body. It had more than ten years since she and Lizzy started the place together. Her late Uncle Henry had passed the business on to her, complete with yearly lease on the space, after she'd worked by his side for the previous twelve years. Then, she turned right around and invited in Lizzy, the only other lesbian she knew who could capably find her way around an engine.

This was Tenika's dream—a woman-owned garage. She saw Driven as a kind of hub for women, a place where their concerns would be listened to and respected, no matter who they were or what they were driving. And she was clear that she didn't want to run it alone, no way no how, because Tenika knew she was more of a collaborator.

Enter Lizzy.

At the time, Lizzy was working for a high-end foreign motors garage, and while the money was pretty good, the all-male atmosphere was getting to her. She and Tenika had connected over the years, having a beer now and then and talking shop. And Lizzy had filled in at one point when Tenika broke her arm. Uncle Henry had been suitably impressed. After he suddenly succumbed to a massive heart attack, Tenika spent the next three months trying to run the old garage by herself.

Finally, she gave up and called Lizzy.

Together they created something entirely new. They pooled their resources; paid the insurance and taxes; and bought new signage, stock and advertising space. Together they weathered learning about hybrids and electric car batteries, and all manner of interior wiring systems. And through all of it, they worked smoothly and easily in their own particular rhythm.

Again and again, they'd gladly taken the risk. The reward was a pretty much constant stream of women just like them—dykes with car issues. Tenika just loved that. Theirs was a community completely centered around queer women and their cars. She figured Uncle Henry would have been proud.

This was her baby now, her retirement plan and her joy in life. And she'd be damned if some chick with chair massages and a sushi chef was going to bring them down. *She can just try*, Tenika thought as she snapped on the coffeemaker a little too aggressively. In that moment, her competitive ire started to course through her blood once again, extinguishing her fear.

Good, she thought. Because she might need to kick some ass, something her business partner was definitely incapable of.

Now Tenika noticed the blinking light on the answering machine, indicating a message. She pressed the button and it sputtered a little. But then, slowly, the lone message played beneath a layer of static.

"Hey, ladies, it's Bernard. Call me. We need to talk."

Now a new surge of adrenaline pushed through her body, and Tenika felt her gut twist. Bernard was the landlord and this was not a good sign. "We need to talk" was probably code for "I'm evicting you."

Stop it, she cautioned herself. Bernard had never given her the feeling that their lease was in jeopardy. All she had to do was stay positive, and the rest would sort itself out.

Still, Tenika feared Lizzy's arrival, which was bound to happen at any moment. Poor Lizzy. Salt of the earth. A good soul if there ever was one, and a believer in always doing the right thing. The fact was that Lizzy had been in a funk for nearly a year. And if Bernard's call was what she feared, this might push her right over the edge.

Okay, Tenika cautioned herself, *just be cool.* Even if it was an eviction, she and Lizzy were solid business partners and they'd get through it. They were like yin and yang or salt and pepper, and they capably fixed every last car that rolled in. They had a mission, a larger purpose, and it didn't matter one damn bit that Lizzy was a forty-something and Tenika was in her mid-fifties, or that Lizzy was East Coast and Tenika was born and raised in Oakland. Nor did it matter that Lizzy was white and she was Black.

At the end of the day they were sisters, pure and simple. Sisters who were here to fix their other sisters' cars.

And they would succeed, no matter what it took.

*

Lizzy Edgewood lay on her back staring at the ceiling. She knew she had to get up. She'd known it for more than an hour, since her highly annoying alarm clock began its electronic bleat.

She hated this particular day. Lord, how she hated it. On this day, exactly one year earlier, she was shown the door by her last lover, the beautiful and somewhat dangerous Rebecca. And here she was, still feeling immensely sorry for herself.

Rebecca, meanwhile, had moved to L.A., gotten an album deal and was now living with the high-profile music video director who'd shot the video for her first big single, "You Suck (The Breakup Song)." Naturally it had gone viral.

Lizzy hoped they'd be deliriously happy together.

So what did it matter if she got up, put on her coveralls, made her sandwich and rode her bike to work? There weren't any jobs on the books anyway, save for the tire rotation that her chiropractor's cousin needed. Tenika would undoubtedly have it done by the time Lizzy arrived.

Today was just going to be another very slow day. Lizzy could feel it. And she could feel the pep talk her well-meaning business partner would give her as soon as she walked in the door. Staring at the ceiling for a moment longer, Lizzy closed her eyes and replayed Rebecca's final, stinging rebuke for the thousandth time.

"It's that fucking garage you love…not me."

Once more, Lizzy pushed against the intrinsic pain that surrounded her like a cloud. Pulling back the covers, she got out of bed and trudged toward the shower. In the end, she knew she just needed to keep moving.

*

"Kate?" yelled Mindy Rose, sinking just a little more deeply into the whirring hot tub. "You there?" She waited expectantly, but there was silence.

"Oh, Ka-aaaaty!" she called a little more robustly, her voice rising up into a cute parody of a child calling her mother. She didn't care that Kate might not be awake yet, or ready to be pressed into service.

But then, that's how Mindy Rose was. Mission-driven.

Still there was no sign of Kate. "Don't make me get out of the tub!" she yelled a little more darkly. "Please!" she added in a faux attempt at courtesy.

A moment later, the door to Kate's balcony opened and her assistant appeared, clutching her bathrobe closed. Kate was not a morning person. She looked down at Mindy Rose sleepily, blinking against the morning light. "Sorry," she said, with a yawn. "I couldn't…were you calling me?"

"Good morning! Could you be a total sweetheart and make me lemon water, room temperature, in a quart jar? And add a teaspoon of Celtic sea salt?" Mindy Rose's voice rose up in a slight question, as if to make her demand just a wee bit more innocent. Then she added the phrase she used all the time, as if it were some kind of auto-pass for poor conduct. "Thanks, love."

Kate just looked at her blankly for a moment.

"I think my electrolytes are off," Mindy Rose explained, switching off the jets in the tub. Once more she sank back into the steaming water. "Thank you!" she called, dismissively.

Kate turned away wordlessly and slipped inside. *That girl is clearly losing her edge*, Mindy thought to herself with annoyance. Maybe it was time to ship her back to County Cork, or wherever in God's name she was from.

But hiring personal assistants truly was such a pain in the ass. Furthermore, Mindy knew she needed Kate just as much as Kate needed her. Seven years of devotion had left their mark. Mindy closed her eyes and tried not to think about it.

Instead, she focused on her positive thought for the day: Margins. Today she would go through her books and review the projected profit margins for the garage. So far things were humming along nicely. Customers from the lesbian list serves were already pouring in, and they'd only been open for a week. As predicted, the chair massages were already a big hit. Only the sushi bar remained unfinished, though Kate promised her the sushi chefs would start any day.

This was it, Mindy Rose thought with satisfaction.

Her new life—the life she'd thought about for thousands of miles around endless racetracks was finally here. She was done with being tightly strapped into a one-hundred-degree hothouse on wheels, hurtling through space at 200 mph. She was finally done with sanitizing her personal life to make it palatable to the big money sponsors from the deep south. The fried chicken chain, the Christian bookstore, the tire manufacturer—they could all go to hell now.

They were the ones who couldn't wrap their heads around a lesbian spokeswoman, but their customers clamored for her and her non-stop wins. So, Mindy Rose pretended to be straight for all those years. The public bought it willingly.

And now? Well now she could be whoever she effing well pleased. She'd earned it. Her one remaining client, a kiddie-play-land-pizza chain, seemed grudgingly comfortable with the fact that she was gay.

Yeah, okay, fine. She missed driving. At least, she missed it a little. But it wasn't the driving that was hard to let go of. It was the stature, the publicity, the glare of the lights that really buzzed Mindy Rose. It was being stopped in drugstores, movie theaters, restaurants. It was signing the autographs and the TV contracts. And the big checks were pretty nice, too.

But all of that would come back. Mindy Rose knew it, for she was never very far from the spotlight. Her dad had trained her well way back in the karting days to find it. And once she did, she never let it go.

"Kate?" she commanded once again, her voice rising a little. "Hello?"

A moment later her assistant appeared, still in her bathrobe, now carrying the requested quart of salted lemon water.

"You used the Meyer lemon in the fridge?"

"I did," Kate answered evenly. She refused to look Mindy in the eye as she handed over the jar. "Is there anything else?"

Mindy eyed her carefully. "What's up with you?"

Kate glanced at her boss. "Nothing," she replied. "Nothing's up. Why?"

"You just seem…I don't know…" Mindy Rose cocked her head, studying the Irish woman. "I mean, you have everything you could possibly want, Katy. You've got a lovely room in a very nice house. We're not on the road anymore. We're here, and we're doing this business we've talked about forever. So what the hell is it?"

"Oh, it's all very lovely, Mindy. I'm certainly very lucky indeed," concurred Kate. She studied the steaming water of the hot tub. "It's getting late. I need to get dressed," she murmured.

"Aren't the sushi chefs starting today?"

Kate nodded affirmatively. "Must run," she said, backing away.

Mindy watched her go almost curiously, as if she were inspecting an insect trying to fly with a broken wing. "See you at the garage," she called, to which Kate raised a passive hand as she retreated up the stairs to her room. "Oh, and hey, walk Mr. Big before you go."

"'K," she heard Kate reply as the door to her room firmly shut.

Something was definitely up with that girl, Mindy thought. But really, at the end of the day, what did it matter?

She was here now, living in her dream house, soaking in her tub. There was only one way to go and that, undoubtedly, was up.

Chapter Two

Kate Morahan was a terrible liar. That was the real problem.

Not only was she unable to hide her dissatisfaction from Mindy, who was definitely on to her, but she lived in almost constant fear of being busted by ICE. If she ever got that knock on the door demanding to see a green card, or any proof of her legal residency, she'd probably faint. And then she'd be deported.

Kate walked grimly down the driveway to her car parked just beyond the gates to Mindy's estate. Mindy didn't care that she had an undocumented worker in her business. But then, Mindy generally disregarded rules of any sort. She considered herself a 'special case' to whom the rule of law did not actually apply.

Kate had learned this over the last seven years as Mindy's assistant. "Just do it," was Mindy's rallying cry, which Kate had been able to go along with, generally, in spite of her abject terror of being caught. And in spite of the queasy feeling she got from so many of Mindy's demands.

One could say it was good for her, all this toughening up. Yet, at this point, Kate was simply weary. It seemed all of her life she'd been 'just doing it,' right from the moment she had to serve as a child barmaid in her father's pub when her mother was too drunk to show up.

And, yes, there was this matter of being stuck living with Mindy. She'd been meaning to get a place of her own. She really had. It was just, well, she didn't know what, exactly. Some invisible something stopped Kate every time she got online to search for apartment listings, and it wasn't just the vast expense of renting in the Bay Area.

The fact was that she needed Mindy just as much as Mindy needed her.

That first year when Kate was on her own in the U.S., temping, babysitting and generally doing whatever she could to survive, she hung on by thinking about the beautiful airplane ride that brought her to California. It was the one that took her up and away from the dark confines of her family and their tight, judgmental ways. The relief she felt that day was palpable. The very rightness of that flight was profound. It was as if Kate finally felt safe for the first time in her life.

At the time, she had a thousand dollars in her pocket and all the assurance in the world that somehow, one way or another, she would finally live life on her own terms. And yet, here she was eight years later, still as uncomfortable as ever.

Somehow, her personal revolution hadn't yet happened.

Kate opened the door to her car and got in. Then she looked up the hill past the big electric gates and considered her current home. It was certainly luxurious, with its rambling garden in the back, complete with beehives and timed sprinklers in all the flowerbeds. Yes, it was very nice, indeed, even if she wasn't allowed to park in the driveway. On paper, it all seemed pretty good.

What was bothering Kate was something far bigger—a kind of an existential unrest. Something kept tugging at her, pulling her in the opposite direction, and its force terrified her. Especially because she had no idea what it was. She was good at her job. Very good, in fact. But that was no longer enough to keep her grounded, calm and compliant enough to meet Mindy's every demand.

Make no mistake, Kate was grateful to Mindy. She'd provided her with stability and a framework of respectability at a critical time. In turn, Kate had served her boss well, providing everything from social media marketing to wardrobe consulting. It was Kate who'd found the space for the All-Star Garage, and Kate who came up with its name.

It was Kate who understood intuitively what would make the local lesbians come pouring through the door, just as Kate knew how to keep the NASCAR sponsors happy back when Mindy was still driving. And it was Kate who worked hard nearly every weekend, and late most every night, keeping this listing ship upright and organized.

The fact was that after seven years of this, Kate had begun to actively hate her employer. Each day she walked down the hill to her faded green Toyota, with its dented bumper and its customized license plate holder, it was just a little harder to ignore what was really going on.

"Give fearlessly, and you shall never want," said the license plate holder. It was something her dear old Gran used to say when she was looking after Kate. Gran was now long dead, but it was a philosophy she'd carried with her to California. Kate was a nonstop giver. Too much of a giver, as it turned out.

Now it just seemed way too idealistic. In fact, it seemed downright silly. Kate had yet to experience the part about 'you shall never want.' It seemed she was always in a state of wanting these days. Mostly, of course, because of Mindy.

Without a racetrack and other drivers to obsess about, Mindy, herself, was out of sorts. Yet, even worse, Mindy suffered from CTE from one too many car crashes. A steady stream of concussions had left her with a hair-trigger temper, and a far more aggressive approach to stamping out the competition.

So now Mindy focused squarely on an aging garage called Driven that had been happily serving the lesbian community for more than a decade. It was Mindy's belief that grinding the competition to dust would not only be necessary, it would be fun.

Naturally it fell to Kate to be Mindy's henchwoman, whether she liked it or not. She'd even been required to dig up information on the owner of the building the Driven Garage occupied, including the man's phone number. Kate agreed grudgingly, mainly because she believed her job depended on it. Then she tried not to think about what Mindy had done with that information.

Kate started the ignition and pulled away gently into the soft fog of another morning in the Oakland hills. She would be fine, she told herself. She had to because there was no other choice.

Once again Kate steeled herself to just get on with it…whatever 'it' might be.

*

"Come on, Lizzy. Don't you start playing that damn violin again," Tenika warned.

"I can't help it!" Lizzy protested. "It's our anniversary—or at least it was. It's like the worst possible day of my life."

In the background, Tenika just crossed her arms and looked at her friend with pointed annoyance.

"That was a year ago. 365 days have passed, Lizzy. 365! While you're busy withering away, the whole damn world is passing by right outside that window. Anyway, I doubt Rebecca's doing any pining over you today."

Lizzy grimaced at the thought. "Yeah, yeah, I know," she said grumpily. "Whatever," Lizzy gazed distractedly around the garage for a moment. "What are we going to do about this place, T?" she asked with a sigh.

It was so quiet in the garage, there were veritable crickets. "We have any appointments today?" Lizzy asked.

"Not really. I finished the tires already." Tenika hesitated. Now was probably not the time to tell her partner about Bernard's call. Still, she knew she had to.

"Uh, Lizzy?" she began.

Lizzy was now inspecting the appointment book as if it might magically fill up before her eyes. She did not look up. "What?"

Tenika was about to tell Lizzy about the call, but she stopped herself. Lizzy's usual butch swagger was gone. Despite her well-worn work boots, her pro coveralls and Black Lives Matter sweatshirt, Lizzy looked like a little girl who had just lost her mother as she stared at the empty appointment book.

"What?" Lizzy repeated.

"Nothing. I just…" Tenika hesitated. Then she cleared her throat. "I brought a little something for the altar. For Ogun, the iron god. Apparently, he makes shit happen."

"Okay," Lizzy said, still flipping through the appointment book. "Great."

Tenika crossed her arms and sighed. "Now look, Lizzy, you've just got to deal. You can't go on wallowing in this self-pity shit forever."

"I know. I know!" Lizzy said, her voice rising. "But I'm telling you, it's hard," Lizzy's voice crumbled slightly. She looked at Tenika and there were tears in her eyes.

Instantly Tenika felt for her. She put her hand on her friend's arm. "I'm sorry, baby girl," she said more softly, giving her arm a pat. "I just hate to see you suffer like this."

"No! I know you're right," Lizzy admitted, wiping furiously at her eyes with the heel of her hand. "It's obvious what has to happen. I just…can't," her voice squeaked. For a moment, it looked like Lizzy was going to break down right there and start sobbing.

Tenika pulled her friend in for a hug. "Now, come on," she said into Lizzy's shoulder. "You got the goods, girlfriend. You just have to give them away is all. You've done all your crying. Hell, I'd be shocked if there were any tears left in there."

"I know," Lizzy sniffed, with an embarrassed smile. She pulled a red bandanna out of her pocket. "I'm sorry," she said, blowing her nose. "This is totally dumb."

"It's not dumb. It's life," Tenika said. "I was in the same sorry shape before I met Delilah, but I had to make a decision to just get on with things. I didn't meet her until I did that. Don't get me wrong, I moped around for the better part of two years. Then someone shook me by the shoulder and woke me up. Now I'm shaking your shoulder, Lizzy. It's your time to wake up." Tenika looked at her business partner sternly.

Lizzy wiped at her face again with her hand. "So, what should I do?" she croaked.

Tenika crossed her arms and looked at her. "Simple. Move on. Like, right now."

Lizzy thought for a second. Then she sighed. "Okay," she said softly. Once more she gave the red bandanna a large nose blow. "There. I'm done crying. You're right. I'll move on."

"Good," Tenika said with satisfaction. They looked at each other for a moment. "Now maybe we're finally going to have a little fun around here."

Lizzy smiled. "I guess I've been pretty boring lately, huh?"

"The worst," Tenika confirmed.

The two women laughed. Then Lizzy cleared her throat. "Were there any calls?" she asked.

Tenika just smiled at her business partner. "Nope," she lied. "Not a one."

*

"Where is Mr. Shin?" Kate asked, looking around the garage for the other sushi chef.

The Japanese man in front of her murmured something unintelligible.

"Excuse me?" Kate leaned in toward him. He'd arrived a few moments earlier for his first day on the job as a sushi chef, and he was most decidedly alone.

"Shin go back," the chef repeated.

"Oh! Back where?"

15

"Japan."

"Japan? He was just here yesterday!" Kate exclaimed. *What the hell?*

"Shin go back. No good."

Kate sighed. She had no idea what was 'no good' or why Shin left, but then what did it matter? This was the problem with hiring people from the Internet. Fortunately, there were always more where he came from.

"We'll make the best of it now, won't we, Mr. Aioki?" she said in her most chipper voice. Mr. Aoki looked at her blankly. "Never mind," Kate muttered. "Follow me."

The uncomprehending sushi chef still looked at her. She could have sworn his English was better when she interviewed him.

"Fish," Kate said, enunciating clearly. "We get fish." The chef's face lit up and he gave a small bow.

"Hai!" he said.

Already the day was going rapidly downhill.

An hour earlier Mindy had declared the massage chairs unusable, insisting they smelled like cheap perfume. "I personally wouldn't want my face anywhere near them," she announced haughtily. Kate had no idea what she was talking about. If they smelled like anything, it was upholstery. But then, her aim was to stay out of Mindy's crosshairs today.

Now, however, it was clear she would have to tell Mindy they just lost one of their sushi chefs. That was certain to get a big reaction. Kate decided to save up her mojo and avoid Mindy for as long as she could.

An hour later, Mr. Aoki was happily installed cutting fish, and Kate began stuffing massage chairs into the back of her car. It would take several trips to Emeryville to return them all.

Suddenly Mindy appeared at Kate's side. She looked like a vintage starlet from a Hitchcock movie. A long silk scarf was draped around her neck, and she wore vivid red lipstick. "Off to lunch with some venture capitalists," she announced gaily. "Hey, when you get back could you do a Yelp campaign for me?"

"A Yelp *campaign*? I don't know what a Yelp campaign is, but I can certainly leave a review for something..."

Mindy smiled. "You are so funny sometimes," she said with a dark smile. She stepped a little closer and lowered her voice slightly. "I want you to leave half a dozen negative reviews on the page for Driven Garage. Just set up some fake accounts."

"Oh," Kate heard herself say in a small voice.

Mindy began to walk away crisply. "But don't worry," she said over her shoulder. "You can do it when you get back."

Stunned into silence, Kate watched Mindy climb into her convertible and back away. For a moment, she fantasized that Mindy's scarf might get caught in a wheel. Perhaps she might even be strangled, just like Isadora Duncan.

Mindy gave a jaunty little wave as she pulled out of the parking lot, and Kate waved back.

Then she closed her eyes, wondering how much worse things could get.

*

"*Sushi in a garage?* Are you kidding me?" Lizzy looked up from the dark interior of the pickup engine in front of her. Things were bad enough that she was now doing maintenance on her own vehicle.

Tenika shook her head. "And chair massages, too. We saw it with our own eyes. Six little massage chairs, all lined up pretty in the window."

"They must be expecting some heavy traffic," Lizzy concluded.

"I think they've already got it," Tenika noted gently.

"What? You think *that's* why we don't have any jobs?"

Tenika nodded affirmatively.

"No, no, no!" Lizzy protested. "I mean, come on, T! We've had the same customers coming in this door for the last ten years.

They love us. They're not all going over to some garage just because they'll give them back rubs and raw fish."

Tenika just shrugged. "They're going somewhere. 'Cause they're not coming in here, that's for damn sure."

Lizzy grew more agitated. "Who is this Mindy Rose chick, anyway? Is she even batting on our team?'"

"She is," Tenika affirmed. "She came out on *Good Morning America* six months ago when she retired."

"And why is she here? Why isn't she in L.A. or something? Or at least San Francisco?"

"Wanted a taste of the good life, apparently," Tenika sniffed. "She couldn't find a big enough space in the city, I imagine, so we're stuck with her...and her fake tits and her chair massages and her sushi frickin' *whatever*."

Lizzy put down her wrench. "Okay," she said. "Maybe I should just go over there and meet this chick." Picking up a nearby cloth, she began to wipe her hands.

Tenika looked alarmed. "Wait, right now? You're going over to Mindy Rose's garage?"

"Sure. I'm gonna welcome her to Oaktown," Lizzy said. "You know, bring her the proverbial fruit basket."

"Oh, I don't know Lizzy. I saw this woman on TV, and she's got a total viper vibe."

"Relax, it's just a little chat." Lizzy looked around for her phone. "I'll be back in a while."

"Wait!" Tenika stopped her. "Don't go over there. I'm telling you, I have a very bad feeling about her."

"What's she going to do, come after me with a wrench?" Lizzy laughed. "You know what's wrong with you, T? You're way too suspicious of other people. You always think the worst about them."

"What do you want? I'm an East Oakland girl. Anyway, why do you need to rush over there?"

"T, come on. It's no big deal. I'm just going to—"

"Bernard called," Tenika blurted.

Lizzy stopped and looked at her. "Bernard? Landlord Bernard?" A look of consternation passed across Lizzy's face. "Why didn't you tell me?"

Tenika sighed and hesitated. "He says he 'needs to talk to us,'" she said, emphasizing his message with air quotes.

"Jesus," muttered Lizzy. "I need this right now like a hole in the head. We paid the rent, right?"

"Of course."

"Then what the hell does Bernard want?" Lizzy asked rhetorically. "You want me to call him?"

"You or me."

"I'll do it," Lizzy sighed. Picking up the garage phone, she began to dial his number. "You'd better get over to that altar and start to pray, T, 'cause the time for reinforcements is now."

"Yup," Tenika said quietly, taking up her position by the offering to Ogun.

Bring it, Mother Earth, she silently prayed. *Help us get through this and whatever else might be ahead.*

A moment later Lizzy hung up the phone. She sat back in her seat at the counter, not saying a word. She was just staring at the counter.

"So?" Tenika called across the garage, but Lizzy didn't answer.

She walked toward her partner, who now sat in a posture of total defeat on the same grimy chair she'd been swiveling on for a decade. The silence continued.

"Lizzy?" Tenika pressed. "Talk to me."

Lizzy looked up at her, and she was visibly pale. "They're doubling the rent, T. We have two weeks to sign a new lease or we have to get out."

Tenika felt the pit of her stomach give way, and the two of them now fell silent. For once, Tenika was glad they were alone in the garage.

"Some fucking yerba mate factory wants to move in here," Lizzy explained.

"Okay," Tenika said uncertainly as she processed the information.

"Okay? *OKAY?*" Lizzy yelled. "This is not 'okay', T. This is ridiculous! This is the whole goddamn problem with the East Bay. Everything that's real is dying on the vine. Everyone who built this town is being forced out. It's all turning into one giant feelgood corporate mall…with fucking sushi bars and chair massages!"

"Agreed," Tenika said. "What the hell is yerba mate?"

"It's some Peruvian jungle tea," Lizzy said darkly. "It makes you feel happy to be alive and shit. Rebecca was all over it. Naturally!"

"Easy…" cautioned Tenika.

"And now those fuckers want to take our garage. I mean, why is this even happening? We've run a rock-solid business for years—always in the black! Always! We have our people!"

"No one's taking our garage," Tenika said firmly.

Lizzy looked at her. "How do you know?"

Tenika sniffed derisively. "Because we have not begun to fight yet, girlfriend. And I know you and I know me, and we are not going to put up with this horse shit. Nor are we going to go waltzing straight into the lion's den."

"Okay, fine," said Lizzy. "But we'd better think of something fast. Because, basically, we need a miracle."

"I'm down with that," replied Tenika, and then a slight smile crossed her face. "This is the thing about the human race, Lizzy. We always get what we need in this life. And you and me? We need this garage. And so do all the women we're here to help."

Lizzy gave a sigh. As usual, the prophet had spoken.

She just hoped to hell Tenika was right.

Chapter Three

Two hours had passed and Lizzy was now pacing the perimeter of the garage like a caged animal. They'd floated and killed at least half a dozen ideas, including obtaining a new line of credit. Tenika wasn't one to borrow her way out of problems.

No, in her mind at least, this was a challenge that would only be solved by simple ingenuity and a good dose of survival instinct. If Tenika knew anything, it was that their innate drive to succeed was their best defense against failure.

"All we need is one good idea, Lizzy," she declared. "Just one. But it's got to be a killer idea."

Lizzy stopped her pacing, and looked up hopefully. "Maybe we should get a cappuccino machine."

"What, you're going to start making lattes in the garage now? Are you even listening to me?" Tenika asked, her voice rising.

"Other businesses do it. What about all those convenience stores and gas stations? They make a killing on snacks."

"We are not a gas station," Tenika protested. "And we're not selling some damn Twinkies."

"I'm not saying Twinkies—I mean, what if we sold coconut water...or weed? What if we got a dispensary license?" Lizzy's eyes lit up. "If they can do sushi, why can't we do pot brownies?"

"Sounds simple to pull off in two weeks," noted Tenika, dryly. "Anyway, do we really want people to drive out of here stoned? I see regulatory issues here, sister."

"Yeah, okay. Bad idea," Lizzy admitted. She scanned the garage around her for the thousandth time that morning, trying futilely to see it with new eyes. "I don't know," she said miserably. "There's just something missing. Some kind of...*something*."

"Cleaning up the place and painting it could certainly help," Tenika said. "I mean, Lizzy, the place is a mess. It's like some guy's garage. All that's missing are the pinup girls in the bathroom."

"Hey, maybe that's an idea," Lizzy murmured, half to herself.

Tenika silenced her business partner with a look. She picked up the impact wrench and headed back toward Lizzy's pickup. "I'm going to try to get some work done."

"You're probably right. A coat of paint would help," Lizzy continued.

Tenika peered inside the truck engine. "Couldn't hurt," she agreed, without looking up. "But you and I both know it's not enough. You looked at these valves?"

"Yeah," Lizzy sighed. "They need replacing. But, T, hear me out. Painting the place would at least help us get our heads on straight. It's therapeutic. All that rolling." Lizzy walked around, her hands on her hips, surveying the walls around her. "Yeah, even just a nice clean coat of white paint. A little semi-gloss..."

"It'll look clean. Then what?" Tenika countered. "Our competition is chair massages and a sushi bar. We've got to think bigger."

The two women looked at each other in dismay. It seemed almost certain they were screwed.

*

Kate sat in traffic at the MacArthur Maze, an ornate tangle of highway spaghetti that somehow sorted cars into eastbound and westbound traffic. The Maze was almost always at a standstill, regardless of the time of day. She crept forward, heading under a loaded overpass as 80 merged with 580 toward Berkeley and Sacramento.

Around her, the East Bay drivers inched and pushed, inched and pushed. Neither the Teslas pumping Drake nor the Latino gardeners with their beaten-up trucks could make any progress. But there was always relief up ahead, Kate told herself. The stretch past IKEA was usually clear. And, for her next trip with the massage chairs, which would be in less than half an hour, she would definitely be taking surface streets.

Kate resisted the urge to look at her phone as she sat there. Instead she fiddled with the radio knobs. The Soul of the Bay started pumping vintage Jackson 5 into the car.

Bah-bah-bah-bah-bah-BAH!
Bah-bah-bah-bah-bah-bah!

Turning up the volume and lowering the windows, Kate sat back and relaxed. It was a California day. The fog had lifted. The San Francisco Bay was a distant glimmer in the distance, past the cars and the highway, the railroad tracks, and the container ships and the cranes. The sun was warm on her naked arm. Traffic had picked up slightly. *This will all ease up any moment*, she thought to herself.

Perhaps her life would as well. Perhaps some great stroke of fortune would descend upon her like lightning, and she could lose the constant shadow of worry. Perhaps everything would suddenly and magically change.

As Kate predicted, the traffic eased as she rounded the curve coming onto 80. Accelerating, she pulled out into the far right lane. Her lane emptied out as cars sped off in various directions.

As Michael Jackson's baby voice shouted, "Sit down, girl. I think I luuuuv ya!" a loud, hard bang came from the front of the car, and Kate's front end began to weave wildly. Immediately, she hit the brakes. She heard her tires screech as she spun in a perfect slow motion circle, knowing at any moment she was about to slam into the cement barrier at her side.

Bracing herself for impact, Kate intuitively shut her eyes and eased up on the brake. Then strangely the car simply stopped. After a few seconds, she opened her eyes and found the car sitting slightly askew at the edge of the Powell Street off-ramp, as the apparently unfazed traffic whizzed by on her left.

The anticipated crash had not happened. She was, in fact, okay, even if her heart was now beating furiously.

Kate took a deep breath and gently steered the car down the off-ramp, listening to her newly flat tire flap against the road. It was a blowout, she realized. She was going to have to find a garage or a tire place somewhere immediately. It was that or wait for roadside assistance, which wasn't really an option since she had no plan. Nor did she have any idea how to change a tire.

Gingerly, Kate steered the car down a few back streets to San Pablo Avenue. She limped along looking in vain for a garage, until finally she pulled out her phone with a shaking hand. She typed in 'auto garage,' and after a moment the nearest service station appeared.

Driven Garage, 6203 San Pablo Avenue

Of course, she thought grimly. The focus of Mindy's nasty obsession—and her own resistance—was less than 800 feet up on the right. And they would be the ones to fix her flat.

Fine, she thought. *Karma.*

She would get in, get the tire and get out. No harm done. She really did need their help. Kate checked her wallet. She could probably pay in cash, so they would never even learn her name. It would be like a scouting mission, except for the fact that she had no desire to be a scout in Mindy's odious war.

No, what Kate really wanted in this moment was to be taken care of grandly. To hand her damaged car over to someone reliable. And then to be treated to a long, deep massage, followed by a luxuriant bubble bath, with perhaps a nice cold glass of a good, oaky Chardonnay in hand. A long hug would be nice as well. She wanted to be taken care of. To be stroked, listened to and understood. And to be respected.

None of which she expected from Driven Garage, of course. It was just that at this particular moment, Kate could do with all of that and more. That, as they liked to say at home, would be deadly.

Kate could see the sign up ahead, a beacon against the sky. 'Driven Garage. Woman-Owned. Woman-Powered.'

Slowly she flapped her way up San Pablo Avenue to meet the next chapter of her destiny.

*

"Hello?" Kate stood uncertainly in the garage door, and her palms began to sweat. Suddenly, she felt awkward, as if her direct association with Mindy Rose was somehow tattooed across her forehead. "May I have a bit of help?" she called into the shadows.

"Sure," said a tall rangy woman, coming her way.

Kate watched as the woman approached. Her shaggy, brown hair lightly fringed the collar of her coveralls. An oval patch on her chest read 'Lizzy.' *Here she is*, thought Kate. One of the actual owners of the place.

In an instant, Kate was taken in. There wasn't anything glamorous or even particularly beautiful about Lizzy. Rather, she was struck by Lizzy's presence. Strong, capable hands. Warm engaging eyes. A solid, mannish energy that was neither male nor female but somewhere deliciously in between. This woman simply felt…safe.

Suddenly, Kate's heartbeat began to race. "Hi," she heard herself say in a small voice. Immediately, she wondered why she was so nervous? Kate cleared her throat, in an attempt to regain control.

"Is this your car?" asked Lizzy, heading out to the sidewalk. "You've got a flat," she said.

"I just had a blowout near the Maze," Kate explained.

"On 80?" Lizzy asked. Kate nodded. "Whoa," she murmured, then she shot Kate a long, sympathetic gaze. "You okay?" she asked.

"Me? Oh, heavens yes!" Kate felt flustered. "Car's not so well, I'm afraid. Well, the tire's not. She started going completely arseways, you know? But she righted herself."

"Arseways?" Lizzy wondered aloud as she crouched to take a look at the decimated tire.

"Going this way and that," Kate explained. "Swerving."

Lizzy nodded, glancing up once more to take her in. Now Kate intently studied the concrete floor of the garage, trying to still the ever-wilder beating of her heart.

"Well, I'm glad you're okay," Lizzy continued smoothly as she turned back to the tire. "Blowouts can be bad business." She continued with the professional rundown. "You got the sidewall busted out. Combo of worn tires and overloading the weight. What's in here, anyway?" she asked, peering into the back of the car.

"Nothing," said Kate, quickly. "Just, you know, moving a bit of furniture is all." Immediately Kate was glad she'd wrapped the massage chairs up in moving blankets.

"Ah," said Lizzy, gazing at Kate one more time. Kate, meanwhile, was smiling intently at the tire.

Why won't she stop looking at me? she wondered to herself.

"We'll have to replace it," Lizzy continued. "Sidewall tears can't be patched, you know. Let's see if we've got one in stock." Lizzy was now inspecting the numbers on the sidewall. "What year's the car?" she asked.

"2009."

"Let me see what we've got," Lizzy said.

Kate watched her amble away, as an equally tall African-American woman wearing glasses took her place. "Welcome to

Driven," she said, extending her hand. "I'm Tenika, but people call me T. You had a blowout, huh? You okay? Everything still in one piece?"

Kate nodded. "Yes, fortunately."

"Well, that's good," Tenika said as she began circling the car, inspecting the remaining tires. "You got some worn treads here, sister. But Lizzy probably told you that." She glanced across the hood at Kate. "You need to replace at least three. But if we don't have them, they usually come in 24 hours."

Lizzy now reappeared from the back of the garage, and immediately Kate's heart lurched.

"She needs a full set, or at least three," T called out to Lizzy.

"We'll have to order them," Lizzy responded. "You want to go for a full set? At the very least you'll need passenger side and the two rear tires. This way you'll be much safer behind the wheel. I think you get a little money off on the full set."

"Yes, I imagine that's best," Kate agreed.

Tenika pulled up the stool at the counter now and motioned Kate over. "What's your name?" she asked.

"Marta," Kate said without thinking. *Marta? Where on earth did that come from?* she wondered.

Tenika looked up from the computer. "Marta what?"

"Stone!" Kate said a little too loudly. "Marta Stone. I'll pay cash," she quickly added. She was suddenly dying to get out of there as the riskiness of the entire situation began to sink in. It hadn't occurred to her that she might have to leave her car.

All they have to do is lift those blankets to see the massage chairs, she thought grimly. Then they'd certainly guess exactly who she was. Still, Kate had no choice but to leave the car. Meanwhile, these two were helping her. They were actually helping her. And they seemed as friendly and professional as two garage owners could be.

Kate sighed and tried once more to calm herself. She wondered if they were even aware their business was the target of a vicious attack. She also wondered if they were lovers or if Lizzy was actually single. But then she remembered her mission.

Get in, get the tires, get out. She'd just have to hope for the best and come back tomorrow.

"You can pay tomorrow when you pick up the car," Tenika was explaining.

Kate snapped out of her reverie to pay attention to Tenika. Lizzy was lingering by the counter with her hands in her pockets. She rocked gently back on her heels, studying Kate, which made concentration almost impossible. Kate felt herself grow even warmer under Lizzy's gaze. She looked anywhere but at Lizzy, turning her attention this way and that.

"Where are you from?" Lizzy asked her curiously.

"Ireland," Kate said. "I suppose I have a bit of an accent."

"Yeah," Lizzy said lightly. "I like it."

Kate felt her face redden and her hands begin to tremble. The two business owners couldn't be lovers or she never would have said that. *Why am I even thinking these thoughts?*

Kate felt like she wanted to drop straight through the concrete floor of the garage. Was this some sort of delayed reaction to the blowout, she wondered? Or was she just immediately, oddly attracted to Lizzy?

It had to be the blowout, she decided firmly. Lizzy definitely wasn't her type. And even if she was… Well, she just couldn't be. "Grand," Kate said, taking the garage's card from the counter and slipping it into her pocket. "I'll be back tomorrow."

"Great," said Lizzy, arms now tucked up under her armpits.

Tenika looked up from the computer screen in front of her. "We should have it ready to go by 10 a.m."

Lizzy now sprang into motion. "Oh, wait! Do you have a way to get home? Let me drive you."

"Oh, no, no, no!" Kate protested. "No need to trouble yourself, really. I'll just get an Uber."

"No trouble at all, let me take you," Lizzy stepped forward insistently. "I want to!" Her last comment hung in the air between them, suspended for the briefest of moments.

"Uh, Lizzy?" Tenika said gently. Lizzy looked over at her partner, who jerked her head toward the truck they'd just been working on. Its hood was wide open and pieces of the engine were arranged on the floor around it.

"Oh," Lizzy said abruptly. "I, uh…" A sheepish grin moved across her face. "Yeah, I'm afraid I actually can't. That's my truck over there. But Tenika can take you. Can't you, T?" she asked. Lizzy didn't even turn back to ask her partner. Instead, she remained focused on Kate. "I mean, you need to get home, right? Or work maybe? T'll take you anywhere…"

Before Tenika could answer, Kate backed toward the entrance. "No need! No need at all to drive me! I'm just fine on my own and I'll see you all tomorrow. Lovely day to you both and many thanks!" She waved before quickly stepping out the door.

Outside, Kate hit the sidewalk and walked furiously, not slowing her pace until she was three blocks up San Pablo. Looking around, she suddenly realized she had no idea where she was or where she was going. Slowing, she pulled her phone out and opened the Uber app. A car would be along in seven minutes.

What is my problem? she thought as she waited for her driver. She could barely even look at Lizzy, she was so…so…

Interesting? Intriguing?

No, Kate thought grimly. She could barely look at Lizzy because she was so unbelievably sexy. And not in the usual slick, put together way. There was something incredibly unique about her. And there was something else there as well, something subtle. A thread for Kate to follow, a path back to some intrinsic part of herself that had been lost for a very long time. Perhaps ever since she'd left Ireland.

"Do you have a way to get home?" Lizzy had asked.

Kate mulled their conversation over as she waited on the corner of San Pablo and Alcatraz for her Uber to arrive.

Nothing is going to happen, she chided herself. Not if she wanted to keep her sanity, her job and her so-called life. Anyway, a woman like Lizzy most certainly had a wife or a partner. Lizzy was just another face in the great, passing parade of the East Bay.

I simply need some sex, and to have some fun, she decided as she stood there on the street corner, waiting patiently.

She just needed to get back in the game.

*

"Apparently someone had their Lucky Charms this morning," remarked Tenika as they watched Kate make her way up San Pablo.

Lizzy looked at her innocently. "What?"

"*What's that accent you have? I like it*," parroted Tenika. Then she gave a cackle. "I swear, you just came back to life, sister."

"What are you talking about?" Lizzy protested. But now she was smiling. T, as usual, had her number.

"You're into that woman. You've got the hots for Ms. Marta Stone," remarked T. "Now the big questions—Is she single? Is she even gay?"

Lizzy waved her hand as if to erase everything Tenika just said. "Oh, come on! I was just being friendly. Doing the 'customer service thing.'"

"That was some pretty extensive customer service," Tenika replied. "Offering to drive her home? When's the last time you did that? Then volunteering me? You know exactly what you were doing back there, Lizzy."

"Hey, she could have gotten killed out there!" Lizzy countered. "I was just…being protective."

Tenika smiled. "And if she happens to have pretty strawberry blonde hair, little twinkly blue eyes and that cute little Irish accent, not to mention a great pair of legs?"

"Okay, okay! Enough of this!" Lizzy said, slightly embarrassed. "Anyway, you keep encouraging me to date someone..." Her voice trailed off.

"I knew it!" Tenika cried in triumph.

"Yes!" Lizzy exclaimed. "Fine, I admit it! I'm attracted to Marta. For the first time in a year, there's a spark, okay? She's completely charming. And tomorrow she's going to come in here and pick up her car, and I'll never see her again."

"Now, now," warned Tenika clucking her tongue. "Don't start down that road. You are in control here."

Lizzy blinked at her partner. "I am?"

"Well, girl, who else is running your damn life?" Tenika crossed her arms. "I can't believe the things I've got to explain to you. It's up to you to make the opportunity, Lizzy. How'd you get any other woman you've dated?"

"That's true," said Lizzy reflectively. "But, T. She's a customer! I totally can't date a customer."

"Can't or won't, girlfriend?" Tenika responded. "You've got a golden opportunity here. Gol-den. And if you blow it..." Tenika just shook her head.

"Well, she's probably not even gay," Lizzy concluded, darkly.

"Oh, she's a lesbian, all right. I'll prove it to you." Tenika pulled her phone out of her pocket and immediately began combing through Facebook for Marta Stone. She looked up after a moment. "She said her last name was Stone, right?"

Lizzy nodded.

"Okay, that's weird," Tenika commented. "Apparently she's the only person on the planet not on Facebook."

"Wow," Lizzy said a little dreamily. "Makes me like her even more." She gazed out the window up San Pablo.

"Unless for some reason she's using a fake name," Tenika noted. "I'm just going to do a little research..." She opened her Chrome app.

"T, stop," Lizzy said turning back to her. "You can't force a river, you know? Anyway, you can't ask a woman out on a date after you change her tires. You just can't. It's unethical."

"What are you talking about?" Tenika asked, her voice rising in mild outrage. "This is the first woman you've been attracted to in a year. You don't just throw that away. That's precious!"

"Drop it, T," Lizzy returned to her truck. "Give me the ratchet."

"If it were up to me, I'd say Ogun's just doing his thing," Tenika handed over the tool.

"Whatever," murmured Lizzy as she turned back to the engine.

T smiled. The case most certainly was not closed. Not if she had anything to say about it.

Chapter Four

Kate relaxed into the back seat of her Uber and sighed. She closed her eyes. Something had definitely just happened.

An image of Lizzy making love to her swam into Kate's head. Instantly, their entire dynamic dialed itself neatly into place. In a flash, she understood this was about complete surrender to Lizzy's strength, her kindness and her caring brown eyes. All of which Kate wanted in no uncertain terms.

Kate's eyes snapped open in alarm. *Oh, sweet Jesus.* She really had to stop this nonsense right now.

She was not attracted to Lizzy. *God, no. No way on Earth*, she chided herself. *Too butch, for one thing.*

Mercifully, the driver pulled up to Mindy's garage at that moment. Now she had to contend with her boss. Kate wasn't looking forward to that encounter, given that she undoubtedly looked like a guilty 10-year-old right now, complete with a telltale blush.

Of course, she wouldn't tell Mindy about any of it. It really wasn't any of her business, was it? Except for the fact that suddenly Kate didn't have a car, and the massage chairs were now in enemy territory.

Kate rolled her eyes upward. *God, please help me lie convincingly*, she implored. *Help me get through this conversation unscathed. And help Lizzy, too.*

Help Lizzy, too?

Yes. Help Lizzy, too, she thought firmly. At the very least, she could be kind.

A moment later, Kate pushed through the glass door of the garage. Mindy looked up from her phone. "Where the hell have you been?" she asked a little too casually.

"I'm sorry. I had a blowout," Kate blurted. *Dammit, why am I getting into this?*

But what else could she say?

Mindy returned to her phone. "Oh," she said. "I was wondering."

"I was near the University exit," bluffed Kate. "Managed to roll into a tire place over there, and anyway, they have the car for the night. It was rather dramatic actually," Kate said, mostly for affect. She didn't expect Mindy to reply, and she didn't. Nor did she look up from her phone.

Now Kate began moving toward the rear of the garage, where she hoped to busy herself with cataloging inventory for the rest of the afternoon. This was something methodical she could do, something calming to help her refocus her thoughts. Furthermore, the inventory needed to get done.

"A tire place didn't have your tires?" Mindy asked after a moment.

"What?" Kate poked her head out of the back room doorway.

"You said you went to a tire place. And they didn't have your tires in stock?" Mindy asked. She was staring a hole right into Kate—or at least it felt like it. "Good God, maybe we should go into the tire business, too."

Kate flailed helplessly for a millisecond. "Well, I suppose they did, but you know, it turned out I needed some other bits taken care of…" she faltered.

Again, Mindy looked away. Kate retreated into the back room. "Kate?"

Now Kate froze. The tone in Mindy's voice had grown decidedly colder.

"The Yelp campaign?" Mindy asked. "You're doing it today, right?"

A wave of relief descended over Kate. It was only about the Yelp campaign. *Thank God.* Apparently, she'd lied convincingly.

"Oh, yes." Kate said vaguely.

"We need to get it done," asserted Mindy Rose.

"Right," Kate said.

Now Mindy's mouth took on a grotesque imitation of a smile. It was the face of hostility with a fake grin pasted on top. "Just go do it," she said in an upbeat tone. "Won't take long." Once more, Mindy returned to the soul-sucking void of her phone screen.

Kate stepped into the inventory room, and shut the door. Then sitting down, she began to weep. What in God's name was she even doing here?

Yet how on Earth could she possibly leave?

*

"I think we can get our people back. We can get all of them," declared Tenika as the bartender handed her a tall, dark glass of Obsidian stout. She took a sip, closed her eyes and for a moment she was silent, savoring the cold blast of alcohol, chocolate and espresso as it moved across her tongue. "Damn," she said softly. "I love this stuff."

"Right?" Lizzy agreed as she raised her own glass of stout. "To hope," she toasted.

"I hear that," Tenika concurred as they clinked beer glasses.

"Once we get some fresh paint on the place, things will look up," Lizzy reiterated.

"Amen, sister," Tenika said. "Except that that's not enough." Suddenly a smile lit her face. "Hey, baby!" she called across the bar.

A beaming, voluptuous woman with Betty bangs was moving rapidly toward them. She was carrying a small basket, its contents tied up tightly in a cotton bundle, and wore a vintage fifties swing skirt. Its China blue fabric was printed with images of London—red double-decker buses, Big Ben, black taxis and Underground signs. Her tank top revealed her creamy décolletage and an elaborate black and white sleeve tattoo that spanned from her shoulder to her elbow.

The tattoo depicted a poem written in script within a wreath of large, perfectly shaded orchids, highlighted with white. "You know you're in love when you can't fall…" it read, the words trailing off behind an orchid.

"Here you go," Lizzy said, rising and offering Delilah her barstool.

"Don't mind if I do," Delilah said with a smile as she settled herself in. She put the basket primly on her lap then she smiled at Tenika. "Hi, honey."

"The usual?" Tenika asked, leaning in for a kiss.

"Mmm-hmm," Delilah answered.

"How you doing, Delilah?" Lizzy murmured after giving her a brief hug.

"I'm fine, but you seem troubled, Lizzy," Delilah observed. "What's up?"

Tenika ordered a whiskey sour, then she turned back to Delilah. "You got any good ideas on you?" she asked.

"Otherwise we're shit out of luck," Lizzy added. "Some joker wants to turn our garage into a yerba mate factory. We've got two weeks to come up with a whole lot more business, or we're closing down."

Delilah sat forward with a jolt. "Wait a minute, what? Closing down! Your landlord can't just do that!"

"Oh, indeed he can," Tenika told her. "And he is, unless we can stop him. That fancy-ass race car driver downtown has been stealing our business. And, now the rent's mysteriously going up. We've got to get our girls back, like now."

"What the fuck?" Delilah was in shock.

"What the fuck, indeed," replied Tenika.

The three women sat in stony silence for a moment. "I can't believe this," Delilah said softly, trying to process the news. "It's… it's…" Her voice trailed off.

"We're going to paint the place and spiff it all up," Lizzy said firmly. "Clean it up over the weekend. It's gonna be beautiful."

"Yeah, and like I said, Lizzy, it's not enough," Tenika added.

"How do you—" Lizzy started to protest, but Tenika cut her off.

"I know," she said definitively.

A weary smile crossed Lizzy's face. "Marketing isn't really my strong suit," she admitted.

"So play a gig at the garage, then. People will come," Delilah announced. "They love The Breakdowns, Lizzy."

Lizzy's eyebrows shot up, and she looked at Tenika. Lizzy's band played the old soul covers of R&B masters like Sam & Dave and Stevie Wonder. Lizzy herself served as the band's 'broken down blues singer' as she liked to say. And indeed, her rough, low textured voice cut to the heart of the matter every time.

Lesbians from all over the city showed up whenever The Breakdowns played. It seemed they were always up for that time-honored East Bay ritual, the lesbian dance. Furthermore, The Breakdowns were long overdue for another show. There simply hadn't been time lately to book gigs.

"So you think we should play at the garage?" Lizzy asked.

"Sure," Delilah replied. "Why not?"

Tenika and Lizzy looked at each other once more. "But we'd have to paint the place first," Lizzy said.

"Not necessarily," Tenika countered. "Let's do it on Thursday night."

"This Thursday night?"

"Sure, we don't have a whole lot of time" Tenika said. "And we can certainly do a first stab at cleaning up by Thursday. All you have to do is get the band to show up. Oh, and you can invite your new sweetie to the dance."

Delilah's eyes widened. "Wait, Lizzy's got a new lover? What *didn't* happen today?"

"I don't have a new lover!" Lizzy protested. "I just met a woman."

"What woman?" Delilah persisted.

"Some Irish chick. She came in with a blowout," Tenika explained. "She paid cash. Says her name is Marta Stone, but I'm not so sure. What Irish person is named Marta? And is Stone even an Irish name? Anyway, she's not on Facebook."

"Every single person in the world doesn't *have* to be on Facebook," Lizzy scoffed. "Anyway, she's a sweetheart. How can you even think Marta's lying? She exudes goodness."

"Lizzy's already gone," Tenika said, nudging Delilah.

"I'm not gone!" Lizzy argued. "She's a very attractive woman. You encouraged me to date her, T."

"I did indeed," Tenika said with a smile. "Which is exactly why we should have that dance on Thursday night. It will give you a chance to see her again. You said yourself you can't ask a client on a date, but you can sure as hell ask her to a 'special event' at the garage. That's simple enough, right?"

"Hell, yeah!" encouraged Delilah.

Lizzy folded her arms uncertainly. "Really?"

"Don't make me beg," Tenika said darkly, taking a pull of her stout. "This is the first halfway decent idea that's come up all day."

"Okay, okay! Let me start texting some people and see what we can make happen," Lizzy conceded. Then she turned to Delilah. "You don't think it's weird if I ask her to the dance?"

"Please! She's going to see you at your best, Lizzy," Delilah said. "You get up there and start playing, and you know what happens. The girls always start to swoon."

"And you think they'll come see us at the garage?"

"Why not?" Tenika asked. "It's something new and different. This will definitely bring our girls back. At the very least, we can tell them all what's going on."

"Good idea," Lizzy agreed. "I guess I *will* ask Marta."

To Lizzy, the prospect of singing for Marta was both exciting and terrifying at the same time.

But perhaps this was a good sign.

*

Somehow, Kate had successfully managed to avoid Mindy's Yelp campaign all afternoon. First, she inventoried the hell out of the back room. She moved through it like a dervish, feverishly writing down part numbers and photographing part label after part label.

Tireless work appeared to be the only way Kate could soothe her spinning brain.

Now she was sitting down to a much less enjoyable task, but necessary all the same—applying for Mr. Aioki's HB1 visa. Even though he was a sushi chef, he'd managed to hang out in the United States as a student for quite a few years now. Mindy now insisted that they hire him legally, even though she had never offered Kate the same legal protection.

Kate spread the freshly downloaded Form I-129 Petition for a Nonimmigrant Worker, H Classification Supplement to Form I-129 and H-1B Data Collection and Filing Fee Exemption Supplement out on the desk. The documents swam together in a bureaucratic blur.

A wave of bone deep weariness passed through her. This was not good. Taking a deep breath, Kate picked up her pen and tried not to feel the old stab of insecurity that began whenever she thought about immigration and her own uncertain status. Her stomach tightened into its usual, predictable knot.

Slowly, Kate began to fill out the form on top, willing herself to keep going and ignore her own discomfort. Mindy was just doing what Mindy always did, she told herself. Mindy was just focusing on the micro parts of the business while ignoring the bigger picture. That was most certainly why she never bothered to get Kate the legal status she needed.

In fact, Kate was pretty certain Mindy had forgotten altogether that she was an undocumented worker. *You're taking this way too personally*, she chided herself. Such thoughts wouldn't get her anywhere.

In the space marked applicant's name, Kate neatly wrote in Mr. Aioki's name. She carried on filling in all relevant details, ignoring the lingering ache in her gut.

"What are you doing?"

Kate looked up. Yet again, Mindy was checking up on her. "Doesn't look like a Yelp campaign to me," Mindy remarked, tartly. She had a look of annoyance on her face.

"I'll be getting to that in just a moment," Kate lied. "You know how long it takes to process all the paperwork for the visas."

Mindy folded her arms and looked uncertainly at Kate. "I could swear you're avoiding the Yelp campaign," she said.

"Why on earth would I do that?" Kate asked with her best semblance of a laugh.

Mindy drew herself up in the doorway and glared at her. "You tell me," she replied. "All I know is that it isn't happening. No matter how often I ask."

A stab of adrenaline rushed through Kate, as she looked back at her boss. What the hell was she going to say now? Mindy was definitely on to her. It was as if her encounter with Lizzy was now written all over her.

"Mindy, please," she implored. "I'm sure I'll get to it very soon. Immediately, in fact," Kate faltered, trying to keep the panic out of her voice. "We really have to—"

"Show it to me before you leave the garage tonight," Mindy interrupted. "I'll be in my office waiting."

*

Disaster, Kate thought bleakly, twenty minutes later as she studied the blank 'Write a Review' box on Yelp.

She'd pushed around Mr. Aioki's immigration files for a good quarter of an hour before she finally gave up. It was now well past five, and she knew Mindy was, indeed, waiting for her as promised.

Kate had to do the reviews, and she had to do them now. This was her job, whether she liked it or not.

Kate pulled her shoulders back, took a deep breath and began to type a review under the pseudonym, Rosemary Briggs. Then she stopped. Once again, she read the comments Lizzy's loyal customers had left over the years. Naturally, Driven Garage had a five-star rating with dozens of glowing comments.

Like a moony teenager, she gazed at one in particular. "Lizzy has the touch of an artist and the hands of a surgeon when it comes to my fussy Toyota engine. No one else in the city can make her hum quite like this, and so I am and will forever be a loyal fan of Driven Garage."

Kate closed her eyes for a moment, savoring the idea of Lizzy having the touch of an artist. Then she moved on to the concept of Lizzy having the hands of a surgeon. It was almost too much to contemplate at the moment as she noticed a small thrill traveling down her spine.

Stop it. There was no reason to be getting into all of this right here and now.

Who cared if Lucy had the hands of a surgeon? Who cared if Lizzie was strong, powerful and intense?

Who cared that Lizzy kept staring at her when she was at the garage?

Who cared if she had the most beautiful green eyes on the planet?

Just focus on the task at hand, Kate demanded. But her rambling thoughts pressed on, regardless.

"Where are you from?" Lizzy had asked her.

If she was being honest with herself, Kate realized it was almost as if her heart stopped when she stood in the forcefield of Lizzy's steady attention. Then her legs almost gave way when Lizzy told her she liked her accent.

Kate was a goner. She might as well just admit it.

Her eyes moved to the next set of Yelp reviews as she scanned the page. "If it wasn't for Lizzy and Tenika, I don't know what I'd do. They've bailed me out so many times. Once they even let me pay in installments when I lost my job. Everyone knows and respects these two women for a reason. Lizzy and T are the heart and soul of this community."

Kate closed her eyes against the sudden onrush of tears. How could she do this? How could she post a negative Yelp review against a business that was clearly viable, if not excellent? Impulsively, Kate highlighted what she'd already typed and pushed the delete button. Once again, the review box was empty.

Everyone knew how damaging bad reviews were. She couldn't live with herself if she posted even one…and she was probably going to have to post a lot of them. Mindy would almost definitely demand it, given how many five-star reviews Driven had.

"Kate?" Mindy called from her office. "Are they done yet?"

Shit. Kate's hand flew up to the keyboard, and she began typing in the Post a Review box once again.

"I'm almost done!" She lied.

Once again, she began to type. But this time, she typed as tears streamed down her face. Slowly, remorsefully, Kate scrolled down the screen and hit the red button that said 'Post Review.'

There. She'd done it.

Kate blew her nose and dried her tears, as a sad, slow wave of remorse moved through her. For a moment, she put her head in her hands. "Done!" she called, wearily. "I did it."

There was no reply.

Slowly, Kate got up from her desk, and moved to the doorway. "Mindy?" she called. Still there was no answer.

Walking to the office next door, she peered inside.

Mindy had left for the day.

*

Lizzy picked up the black, gritty bar of seaweed soap from her tiled windowsill, and began to soap her forearms. Hot water beat down on her back, her head, her neck and her shoulders, easing the tension that built throughout the day. And what an incredible day it had been.

Lizzy contemplated how it began, with her abject depression over the now forgotten anniversary with her ex. Nothing could seem further from relevant at this moment.

Lizzy began to hum "Stormy Monday" as she lathered her belly and her legs. *Marta*, she thought. Something about her had already gotten under Lizzy's skin, totally and completely. In fact, she couldn't stop thinking about her.

Even with the impending rent disaster that loomed just ahead, Lizzy still couldn't focus. All she could think about was Marta. Tenika was right. She had to make a play for her. She was the first woman to get her motor going in a very long time.

"Wednesday's worse. And Thursday's all so sad," Lizzy sang as she scrubbed at the grease under her fingernails.

A moment later, she yanked back the shower curtain and stepped out of the shower, dripping wet.

"The eagle flies on Friday. Saturday I go out to play. The eagle flies on Friday. Sat-ur-day I go out to play, and I play and I play. Yes, I doooo nowwww…" Lizzy wailed as she toweled herself off.

Lizzy was most definitely planning to play if Marta would let her. She was going to do more than play, in fact. She was going to make love to that woman, and it would be very serious love, indeed.

It would be memorable love. It would be great love! Yes, Lizzy was feeling downright inspired.

By now, a scant eight hours after meeting this new client, she had already forgotten about her self-imposed ban on dating customers.

If Marta would let me…

That was the one unknown. She really couldn't read Marta. She had no idea whether Marta was even into women. But if Lizzy knew anything, it was that she, herself, was too old for unrequited love. Her radar just didn't go off these days unless there was a healthy return coming her way. Chances were that she and Marta were on the same page.

Lizzy hung up the towel to regard herself in the mirror. She wiped away a patch of steam with her palm and her face came into view. Was it her imagination or was she looking older? There seemed to be just a few more fine lines crossing her face than she'd noticed before.

But then, what did she expect? She *was* getting older. Right now it didn't seem to matter one damn bit.

"Gonna kneel down and praaaaaayyyy!" Lizzy wailed as she hung up her towel.

Marta would be hers, one way or another. They were meant for each other.

Lizzy hadn't been so sure of anything in a very, very long while.

Chapter Five

Kate stood in front of the mirror, beating back her anxiety. For a moment, she closed her eyes and simply breathed.

Really there was no need to get all up in lather about this, Kate declared to herself as she took one breath, and then the next. She was simply going to the garage to pick up her car. That's all that was happening. That was it.

There wasn't going to be a date, or even a hint of a date. Such complications would simply push her already tender constitution right over the edge. Once again, Kate reminded herself that Lizzy was nothing more than her mechanic. And that they barely knew each other. Kate really was just there to pick up her car.

She regarded herself in the mirror. So did it seriously matter if her earrings matched her dress? Come to think of it, why *was* she wearing a dress?

Once more, Kate studied herself as she slowly inhaled and exhaled. God, she hated this. She hated the tension of not knowing how Lizzy felt. Or rather, knowing exactly how Lizzy felt and being so nakedly vulnerable that she could scarcely bear to think about it. Still, Kate did not change back into her more comfortable jeans and button-up shirt.

She'd be wearing a dress today. And a very nice one at that.

In less than an hour, Kate would be at the garage. With Lizzy. She would keep her mind on the task at hand—get the car and get out. She would not make eye contact with Lizzy. She would not shake her hand. She would not give Lizzy one single inch of hope, because she couldn't. It really wouldn't be fair.

Except that she would wear a dress because she had to wear a dress. Kate could give Lizzy that much.

Snapping off her bedroom light, she stepped out into the day and shut the door behind her. Mindy glanced up from the kitchen table as she appeared. "A dress!" she declared. "Something special must be happening today."

"No, I was just in the mood," Kate replied as casually as possible.

"Hmph," concluded Mindy, glancing once more at her phone. Then she looked up. "By the way, you've only done one negative Yelp review so far," she noted. "And it was pretty tepid, Kate. I know you can do better."

Kate refused to look at Mindy. Instead, she focused on getting to the back door as inconspicuously as possible.

"The Yelp reviews?" Mindy said, as if speaking to a child. "The smear campaign I keep asking you about?"

"Not my strong suit I guess..." Kate mumbled, reaching for the doorknob. "I'll do more later..."

"Too bad you didn't get your tires done at Driven," Mindy called after her. "Even if you had to drive on the rim. Then you could have included specifics. More believable, you know?"

But Kate wasn't listening. She left so quickly, the door slammed shut behind her. She needed psychic space from Mindy. She wanted to get as far away as she could.

Really, Kate needed an entirely different life right now. Of this, she was acutely aware.

*

"I got up early just to get those tires done," Tenika trumpeted. "I come in the door and boom! You're here and they're already done. This has to be some kind of miracle."

Lizzy looked up from Kate's rear tire with a sheepish expression. "Couldn't help it," she said. "I couldn't sleep."

"That bad, huh?" Tenika said as she put her lunch pail in the mini fridge.

"No, no! Just, you know, spring and shit," Lizzy protested.

"It *is* spring," her partner nodded. "Does all kinds of things to a person."

Lizzy threw up her hands. "Okay, enough of all that, T. Give me a break here."

Tenika looked over with a smile. "I'm just rooting for you, sister."

"Yeah, yeah, whatever," Lizzy groused as she wiped her hands clean. "Anyway, I think Marta wanted the car by nine. Which is, like, now."

"'Marta', yes," Tenika commented. "Or whatever her name is." She moved toward the coffeemaker purposefully.

"I am going to ask her to the show on Thursday night."

"Glad to hear it," T said, nodding thoughtfully. "You've got the band lined up, then?"

"Yep, they're all in. I mean, you're right, T. I can't waste this. I'm into her, I have to admit it. And to let her slip away would be—"

"Excuse me?" A voice interrupted the two women. Lizzy turned around and immediately flushed red.

Here she was, in living color. For a moment, Lizzy panicked over whether Marta heard what she was saying.

Then she did a minor double take on the graceful figure moving toward her, wearing a dress that was as blue as a peacock feather. It was a perfect compliment to Marta's strawberry blonde hair. The linen sheath fit her body perfectly. Lizzy couldn't help noticing that this woman was stunning.

Marta stopped short of Lizzy, leaving a significant gap between them. They both began talking at once.

"Hi, I—" Marta started.

"Are you—" Lizzy interrupted.

Then both of them stopped and laughed. "I'm here!" Marta said almost gleefully. "Assuming the car is ready, of course," she added a bit more soberly.

"It is. Got here early to get her all ready for you," Lizzy told her. "Tires are in good shape. You should be good to go. I even topped off the oil for you, on the house."

"Wonderful!" exclaimed Marta a bit too loudly. Then she collected herself. "Thank you. That's very kind," she added more modestly.

They looked at each other and smiled awkwardly. And Lizzy felt herself dissolve just a little bit more. There was definitely something about this woman—a genuine pull between them. She could feel it more than ever.

Lizzy noticed Tenika discreetly slip away to the back of the garage as the two of them headed over to the cash register.

The paperwork. Yes, Lizzy needed to do the paperwork. She stiffly began to ring up the set of new tires. "Got four tires here… Fireside Stoneluxe whitewalls…serial number 43RTZ6…" she rambled.

Ask her, Lizzy's brain commanded as she typed. *Ask her to the show.*

Lizzy looked up at the beautiful woman in front of her, and suddenly she was tongue-tied. She could say nothing. It was as if her entire nervous system had suddenly seized up.

Just do it. Just go ahead and ask her.

They looked at each other. The silence pressed on between them, heavy with portent.

"Marta?" Tenika interrupted, walking toward them.

The woman did not reply. Instead, her eyes darted around the garage in a futile attempt to avoid looking at Lizzy.

Tenika now appeared directly beside her. "Marta?" she asked again.

Suddenly, Marta jumped. "Yes!" she burst, as if taken by surprise. "I'm sorry. Hello, there."

"Hi. I just wanted to tell you we are having a little event here. Well, a big event, hopefully," Tenika said. "Lizzy's too modest to say, but she's got an awesome blues band. You ever heard of The Breakdowns? Lizzy's the lead singer. They're going to be playing right here in the garage on Thursday night, eight o'clock. Just a free concert for our customers, like you."

"Oh," Marta hesitated. "I, uh, Thursday. Mmm, I might have something on, I'm afraid..." Her words trailed off.

"Don't worry about it!" Lizzy interjected quickly from the register. "We're inviting everyone we work with. Kind of a value-added sort of thing. No big deal," she stressed.

"Right, I wish I could make it, but..." Marta demurred. "I mean, maybe. I'm sure you and the band are quite amazing. I, just..." She did not finish her sentence.

"Oh, she's good alright," professed Tenika.

"T..." Lizzy objected.

"She's hella good!" Tenika persisted more loudly, shushing her partner. "Her band really gets the girls going. Us gay girls like to dance, and we love good music. So everyone shows up. It's a very *good* time. And if you're new in town..."

The woman didn't say anything.

"But anybody can come!" Lizzy suddenly insisted from behind the counter. "You don't have to be a lesbian," she added delicately.

"But I am," Marta suddenly blurted. "Actually," she added, almost as an afterthought.

There was now just the tiniest silence as Lizzy and Marta finally looked at each other. A small depth charge went off between them, and then Marta turned away. *Okay*, thought Lizzy. *Good*. Relief began to flood her body as Tenika did her best to suppress a smile.

"Well, fine then." Tenika said to no one in particular.

Opening her purse, Marta pulled out her wallet, extracted four one-hundred-dollar-bills and laid them on the counter. "Is this enough?" she asked. "I'm sorry, I'd love to come to your show, but I'm not sure I can."

"Of course. Don't worry about it," Lizzy said, picking up the cash. "I was just thinking if you were around. But if not, no problem."

"I'm sure everyone will have a terrific time. And I'm sure the band is amazing," Marta carried on nervously. Her face was apologetic. "Anyway, must get to work." She quickly stuffed the receipt and change into her bag.

"Where do you work?" asked Lizzy.

"Oh, just the other side of town," Marta said hurriedly. "I really have to run." Turning, she headed for the door. "But thank you. I really appreciate it! Great job!" she called over her shoulder.

Lizzy just stood there looking at her go with her hands on her hips.

Marta disappeared from view.

"I don't know, Lizzy," Tenika said, shaking her head. "Something's up with that woman. She's definitely using a fake name." Turning away, she approached the coffeemaker once again. "Four hundred in cash," she remarked. ""Marta', my foot."

Lizzy didn't mind. Maybe Marta was a fake name. And maybe it wasn't. She was definitely gay, though, and Lizzy wanted her. No matter what the hell her name turned out to be.

"Well," she said, shaking her head, "maybe she'll surprise us and turn up."

"Then you'd better damn well get her real name," Tenika said. "Because I'm not going to be picking up the pieces on this one. Consider yourself fully warned."

Lizzy smiled broadly. "I'm warned. And thanks, T," she said to her partner. "You came through yet again."

"I've got your back," Tenika said simply.

Humming, Lizzy moved happily back to her truck with its innards still arranged around the floor.

Marta may have gone, but the conversation was by no means over.

*

Holy mother of Christ.

Kate leaned back in her car seat and closed her eyes at the first stoplight she came to. Picking up her car had been immensely difficult. She breathed deeply, trying to still her frantic heartbeat.

If only Lizzy hadn't been so unreasonably warm and capable of looking right into the very core of Kate's being. Everything would be fine right now.

If only she hadn't noticed the creased edges of Lizzy's coveralls, slightly worn but still perfectly clean. To Kate, this indicated tidiness, steadfastness and a comforting touch of frugality.

If only she hadn't noticed Lizzy's tiny earrings, small studs of a nondescript stone signifying a small but critical bit of feminine energy. If she hadn't seen how carelessly, yet sexily, her dark hair tousled across her brow, or noticed the small tattooed crest of flowers on the back of her wrist, well, then, Kate would be okay.

But she'd observed all of it. And more. As far as Kate could tell, Lizzy was every single last thing she'd ever hoped to find in a woman.

And then to take the bold move of inviting her to an event. One that Lizzy would perform at with her blues band.

A blues singer. Of course. Lizzy *had* to be a blues singer.

Kate sighed. It was all just so over-the-top hot. She really needed to get a grip. The whole idea seeing Lizzy sing pretty much blew Kate's personal wiring.

Now a car behind her honked and Kate's eyes snapped open. The light was green.

Okay. Fine. She'd been here before. There had been other inappropriate women before whom she'd managed to deflect, hadn't there? Kate had valiantly held the line before, hadn't she?

Her mind swam around in circles for a minute, floundering as she drove, until she realized that no, she'd never actually been in this position before. In fact, it had been so long since she'd even been attracted to anyone that she could barely remember what it felt like. Back then it had been casual, furtive sex at college in Ireland, before she'd even come to California.

It wasn't like Kate hadn't tried. She'd been on dates and even posted a profile on a lesbian dating site at one point. But not one of the women seemed a good fit. Some were too plastic. Others too hardcore, and still others too boring. Some had been too inclined to drink, while others talked too much. Gamely, Kate had gone on a few rounds of dates, then she quietly took her profile down.

Kate couldn't even recall if she'd ever been to a lesbian dance. Most of the time, she'd been on the road, touring with Mindy. And that was just an endless string of lookalike T.G.I. Fridays, Pizza Huts and Best Western motels.

Love just wasn't something she was interested in, Kate told herself. Not here and now at this very important juncture in Mindy's business. And certainly not with a woman whose business her boss intended to eradicate.

No. This was simply impossible.

But then Kate could not help but replay the terrible moment in which she announced to Lizzy that she was a lesbian. *Why on earth did I do that?* It was tantamount to waving her hand and saying, 'Pick me!'

Oh God, oh God, oh God, she writhed silently as she drove. *Why, why, why?*

Kate's mind spun wildly now. Why in the hell did she do that? It was only encouraging Lizzy to think she had a chance when there was none. In fact, there was less than a chance. Kate was about to do something that would make her a true pariah to Lizzy.

In mere moments, she would sit down and write up a half dozen more fake smear reviews, forcing Driven Garage to close their doors within a few weeks or maybe months. And, yet...Kate could tell just by standing there in the middle of that garage how much those two women loved their business.

It was evident in the way Tenika circled her car, looking at all the details with such a practiced eye. And in the way that Lizzy talked to her about her blowout. These two women genuinely cared about cars—and especially about their customer's cars. Lizzy had shown up early to change her tire on time and thrown in a free oil change, for God's sake.

How on earth was she going to smear these people? Driven was the last business in Oakland that deserved a single bad review.

A tear now rolled down Kate's cheek, followed by two more. Her chin quivered as she willed herself not to cry. *Crying won't help me now,* she thought with annoyance. Furthermore, Mindy would immediately be in her face, demanding to know what was wrong.

Buck up, she told herself firmly as she parked. She wiped at her face hurriedly with the back of her hand and gave a hard sniff.

You've got work to do.

Chapter Six

"Kate, we're starting!" Mindy's voice crashed in around Kate as she peered at her computer.

Yet again, she'd been sitting motionless, unable to push the 'Post a Review' button on Yelp. She would do it if she could.

She just couldn't.

"Be right there," she called back. Leaning back in her chair, Kate stared at the ceiling. Was she going to do the rest of the smear campaign, or wasn't she? Because if she wasn't, Kate might as well quit right now.

That was the option, of course. Just walk into Mindy's office and lay down her resignation. And then what?

Idly, Kate opened up her online banking account and clicked on her savings account. She had just shy of $7,000. This would last her—with a deposit on a new place to live, first and last month's rent, moving expenses, and general cost of living—maybe a few weeks? Assuming she could even find a place to live.

Once more, the truth settled. Kate couldn't find any way around it; the entire Bay Area was hellishly expensive. And it was impossible to find housing.

Kate looked back at the intractable problem on the screen in front of her and sighed.

The alternative, of course, was to just refuse to do the smear campaign. To just be brutally honest and confront Mindy, and refuse to put up with it anymore. Which would get her fired, she was fairly certain. And then where was undocumented Kate ever going to find another place to work? Once again, her troubled thoughts came full circle.

"*Screw it,*" Kate blurted softly. A surge of wild, reckless anger pushed up inside of her and she stabbed the button that opened up the 'Rosemary Briggs' profile on Yelp. There was the bad review of Driven Garage she'd posted the day before. She hesitated for a moment, her cursor hovering over the digital image of a trash can.

The words sprang up in black and white. 'Delete Post.' Kate clicked it.

Now a message box popped open. "Why do you want to delete this post?"

Because it's patently wrong to lie like this. Because smear campaigns are beyond sleazy. Because I can't be Mindy's little minion any more.

And mostly because I'm dying here.

Kate's eyes scanned the list of radio button choices and landed at the blank box at the bottom. Skipping it, she moved directly to 'Delete.'

"Please select at least one reason," the app insisted.

"Kate, get in here!" Mindy yelled from the conference room.

"Coming," she called, her eyes riveted to the computer screen in front of her.

Okay, fine, Kate thought furiously. She ticked the box next to "I changed my opinion about this business after a new interaction." Then she clicked 'Delete Review' again.

Seamlessly, the app went back to Rosemary's profile page. The errant review was now gone.

Taking a deep breath, Kate felt her shoulders relax for the first time all day. Rising, she realized she would get through this. And no, she wouldn't be doing any more bad reviews of Driven, no matter what Mindy Rose demanded.

Push was, most definitely, hurtling toward shove.

*

"That's what I'm saying," Mindy rambled. "The women are already coming in here. In fact, they're pouring in here, aren't they Jake?"

Mindy's top mechanic nodded. They'd hired Jake away from another area garage a few weeks earlier. "Yep, we're busy all right. And if you're done with me here, Mindy, I need to get back—"

Mindy held up her hand, and tipping her head, smiled at Jake. "I need you here right now, mister. So just stay put," she said, giving him a wink.

Kate still didn't understand why a woman's garage would hire a male mechanic. But then, she still wasn't sure Mindy was even a lesbian. At the moment, it appeared to be more of a marketing niche than a genuine lifestyle.

"Give me numbers," Mindy said, turning to Kate. "What's our total for March so far?"

Kate looked down the list of figures in front of her. "14 repairs, 16 maintenance, two tires," she recited.

Mindy's eyes glistened with delight. "And we've been open how long, Kate?"

"Eight days."

"That's what I'm talking about," Mindy said excitedly. "We've got a good head of steam going here. And once Driven can't afford their lease—"

Kate sat forward. "Wait, what about Driven's lease?"

Mindy looked at her matter-of-factly. "Oh, their landlord is about to close the place. He just jacked up the rent on them. I hooked him up with a yerba mate factory up in Sonoma County that wants to open a new tasting room in the East Bay. Oakland gets yerba mate, and we get the lesbians." Mindy gave her 'cute' giggle. "Win-win, right?"

Kate looked at the papers in front of her on the desk. Was this going to be the moment she protested? When she finally put her foot down and actively rebelled? Kate closed her eyes, measuring the moment. Then she thought, yet again, about her inadequate savings account.

She swallowed hard. "Oh," she said quietly.

"I thought I told you about this," Mindy remarked.

"No, but..." Kate hesitated. "I mean, perhaps it's a bit extreme?" she asked gingerly.

Mindy laughed. "Loser question, Kate. Loser. You want to run with the big girls, you've got to put on your big girl pants. So Jake, you need more guys?" she asked, turning her attention to the mechanic.

He nodded. "That would be great. I could use two or three."

"You know some good ones?" Mindy asked.

"Well, yeah, but they've got jobs."

"Hasn't stopped us yet," Mindy smiled. She stood, put her hands on her hips and surveyed the array of spreadsheets before her. "This is working!" she crowed. "Mindy's All-Star Garage is a hit!" Now Mindy looked up at the others with a victorious smile. "Forward, team. We can't disappoint our fans, now can we?"

Kate said nothing. But her thoughts were going a million miles an hour.

*

Thursday was Vegetarian Night for Mr. Big.

Kate reminded herself of this fact as the stout pug pulled and strained on his leash. He was small, but Mr. Big never ceased to remind Kate who was actually in charge.

They'd barely arrived at Point Isabel and already he was halfway out of the car, whining, scratching and tugging her toward the 'run free' point, where dogs could finally be off leash. "Settle down!" Kate chastened him, but the dog was a snuffling, straining ball of motion, headed for his goal and steadfastly ignoring her. She had no choice but to follow.

A moment later, Kate bent down to remove Mr. Big's leash as they reached the field. "Good riddance," she muttered. She really hated the little dog.

They were having all important 'bonding time' as Mindy put it. She would soon depart for a three-day investor retreat with the firm who was funding her, so Kate would be in charge of Mindy's so-called 'precious bundle,' the aptly named Mr. Big. She took a doggie clean up bag from the post beside her, and put it in her pocket. Mr. Big was sure to do his business at any moment.

Kate wandered along the walking path and the San Francisco Bay spread out before her. Fog had been hanging low over the East Bay all day. By day's end, it had retreated to a soft, pale gray pillow in the distance, pierced by the rust-colored stanchions of the Golden Gate Bridge. The water was impossibly calm before her and fringed by a bank of large rocks. It was like dark glass in which Kate could see herself perfectly.

She felt her frazzled nervous system let go as she sat down on one of the nearby benches. Random dogs meandered by, some running for tennis balls, others obediently following their owners. A golden retriever came up and licked her hand in greeting. The dog gazed at her adoringly and wagged its tail.

Kate stroked the dog's head and looked around for an owner. There was none immediately in sight, but it didn't matter. Point Isabel was a dog community, and the owners were merely friends of the pack. Mr. Big meanwhile was busy pooping a few yards away. Kate got out her bag, and made for the spot.

As she picked up his leavings with her plastic bag-covered hand, Kate's mind drifted back to the entire precarious mess that her life had become in the last 48 hours. She thought about the staff meeting that afternoon and Mindy's casual mention of forcing Driven out of their space. A space, undoubtedly, it would be hard to replace in this market.

Standing, Kate tied the bag in a knot as she stared at the Bay. She wondered if Lizzy and Tenika knew yet about these developments, and for a moment, she considered warning them. It would be the civil thing to do, of course. Not to mention the right thing.

Furthermore, she just plain wanted to.

Only one thing seemed certain, or even hopeful, in the ramshackle ride that had become Kate's life, and that was her immediate and undeniable attraction to Lizzy. The fact was that no matter how many distractions Mindy threw her way, she couldn't, and wouldn't, stop thinking about her.

Her fascination with Lizzy was like her own silent protest; a rebellion of the mind. And it was happening, full-tilt boogie, in the silent recesses of Kate's imagination. In that sacred and enjoyable place, Lizzy had already asked her out, and she'd willingly gone. They'd drunk wine together and talked long into the night. Lizzy had run her hands through her hair. Lizzy had unbuttoned her blouse. And Lizzy had kissed her, slowly, tenderly and with just enough force to make Kate's mind spin.

In the quiet of her imagination, Lizzy had also taken her hand and led Kate away from every last thing that was wrong with her life.

Really, when Kate told the truth about it, Lizzy was front and center in her thoughts. Despite what Mindy Rose was planning, and in spite of her apparent need for her job.

Mr. Big now disappeared up the pathway, running after another pug who suddenly appeared. "Mr. Big!" she called after him, half-heartedly. She wasn't up for running after Mr. Big. Not in her current state. For once, the damn dog could come to her.

To hell with it, Kate thought feverishly. She looked at her watch. It was nearing seven as a peach-tinged sunset flooded the western sky beyond the fog. She should go to Lizzy's concert at Driven tonight. For once, she should just put herself first and do what she, Kate, wanted to do.

Mindy Rose be damned, she thought defiantly. The idea of Lizzy wailing out the blues was something she simply had to see.

Anyway, what was the worst thing that could happen?

Kate sat back and smiled, amused at her own thinking process. "Mr. Big," she commanded loudly to the dog in the distance. "Get over here!"

Mr. Big turned and looked at her, as if considering what to do. Then a moment later, he trotted over to her.

Finally, perhaps, she would take fate into her own hands.

*

Kate's heart began to beat faster as she neared Driven Garage. The entire last hour had been a blur of decision after decision, all made with blinding intensity. Feed the dog. Find the right dress. Iron it. Put her hair up. Take it down. Iron the back of the dress again. Make-up or no make-up? Make-up! Or at least lipstick and mascara.

One task led to the next in a whoosh of adrenaline, and Kate followed giddily, grateful that Mindy Rose wasn't around. All Kate knew was that she was going. She was going! And now, as she actually approached Driven, she reminded herself that her name tonight was Marta.

Or was it?

Perhaps she would just chuck it all and tell Lizzy and Tenika exactly who she was. And what Mindy was up to. Then she would offer her services as an unofficial spy. At the very least, that would give Mindy the kick in the ass she deserved, Kate thought triumphantly.

And, yet...

What if such a move ground all the nice flirty momentum that had been building with Lizzy to a dead halt? Kate reminded herself she didn't really know Lizzy. She might be the sort of person who angered easily. Lizzy might not like her association with

Mindy Rose one bit, as a matter of fact. And she was pretty sure Tenika would positively hate it.

No, Kate had better not say a thing. That would be the prudent thing to do.

For now, at least.

Kate parked halfway up the block and heard the band playing as soon as she stepped out of the car. As she neared the garage, she could feel the bass line rumbling along the sidewalk. Happiness descended through Kate's body as she realized The Breakdowns were actually good. But, of course they were. They were Lizzy's band.

Kate stepped into the open door of the garage and looked around. At least 50 women were dancing in the car bays, surrounded by a sea of auto parts, hydraulic tools and a random stack of tires. Lizzy was up on a platform with five other women—the guitarist, a bass player, the drummer, a sax player and a keyboard player. They were playing an old Aretha Franklin song, "Rock Steady," and Lizzy's voice was unexpectedly low and gravelly.

Kate stood there for a moment, taking it all in. Then she looked at Lizzy…and Lizzy looked at her. She felt it at once—the blessed connection. Kate tried to ignore the heat that was now spreading through her groin.

Lizzy closed her eyes and landed on the next phrase hard. She was singing about being in a car, when you're moving, and her voice spiraled up as the song's driving bass line, the tight engine of the song, kicked in. All around her, women were dancing, the band was in its groove and the air was electric.

This was exactly what Kate had been missing. In fact, this was exactly what she'd been wanting ever since she came to California. It was what she'd imagined back in Ireland, when she lay in bed next to her sister at age fifteen, realizing that she was different from the other girls. Somewhere, she imagined, she belonged.

A young woman with short bangs and an elaborate sleeve tattoo grabbed her hand and pulled her into a tight circle of women who were dancing together. The sax player, a tall Black woman whose long braids swung as she played, was wailing on the riff now. An involuntary smile spread across Kate's face as she danced. She smiled at the simple joy of being alive in this moment, of dancing and bobbing among her people, of finding her tribe, of being part of the group.

She *loved* it.

Kate smiled up at Lizzy and Lizzy smiled back at her and gave a nod of approval. Again, a thrill moved through her. Kate was so glad she'd come.

A moment later, the tune ended, and Lizzy took the microphone out of its stand. "I've got a little announcement to make," she said. "T? Where are you?" she asked. The crowd of women stopped their chatting and listened as Tenika stepped up on stage.

"Thank you all for being here tonight," Lizzy began, after a short shriek of feedback. "So we've got a little favor to ask. You all have known us for a really long time, right?"

The women on the dance floor applauded, and a few hooted their approval.

"Well, there's this thing happening," Lizzy started. But then she faltered, and her voice caught as tears sprang into her eyes. An awkward silence began.

"We love you, Lizzy!" someone shouted as she furtively wiped at her eyes with her hand.

"Umm, the thing is, uh…" Lizzy began again, trying to collect herself. But then she stopped, and a look of crushing sadness passed over her. No more words came.

Kate swallowed hard and found herself unable to look at Lizzy now. She was almost certain she knew what Lizzy was about to say. Meanwhile, Tenika took the mic. "Hey, everybody," she continued smoothly. "What Lizzy's trying to say is that we may have to close the garage in a few weeks."

There was a collective gasp from the audience. Immediately, a swell of murmuring protest began.

"I know," Tenika continued. "I can't believe it myself. The fact is, our rent just got jacked way up, 'cause, hey, this is life in Oakland right now. But I'm saying 'No!' Driven doesn't have to close, girls. We just need y'all to come back and start giving us some love. We need your business. You know we do it all, from your lube jobs to your brand new transmissions. Any little problem you've got with your car, you bring it to us and we'll take good care of you, okay? Just no glass or body work. You with us?"

The crowd applauded and cheered. "You with us?" Tenika asked again. And there was more applause and even louder cheers and whistles from the crowd.

"Are we gonna have to close?" she prompted the audience.

"Hell, no!" someone yelled out, and the rest of the audience cheered.

"Just give us some love, ladies. We're here and ready for you, and we need you. Thank you!" Tenika handed the mic back to Lizzy and stepped off the platform as the crowd applauded and began chanting 'Dri-ven! Dri-ven! Dri-ven!' Immediately, the bass line of "I Wish" took off, and the engine of The Breakdowns began to move once more.

Now Kate threw herself into dancing, which was so much better than reflecting on what had just happened. Better to keep low, keep dancing and get good and sweaty. *Just don't think about it,* she commanded herself.

She looked up at Lizzy, whose face now glowed with the intensity of the music as she sang on about wishing those days would come back once more, and how she loved them so. But still, all Kate could see were the tears she'd shed moments earlier. *Tears.* Lizzy was crying because of Kate's company. Kate's boss. Kate's own actions.

Yet again, she was filled with shame.

She had to stop this now. She couldn't go on pretending her attraction to Lizzy didn't matter and pretending she was some other person named Marta, for God's sake. She had to stand up, do the right thing and tell these people who she was.

She would tell Lizzy the truth tonight, Kate decided. And then she, herself, would finally make a choice.

Was she going to be all in? Even if it meant she'd lose her job? Because just looking around this garage, Kate could already see a thousand ways to improve it. God knew she had ideas. Maybe that would make some kind of karmic reparation for the damage already done.

Kate closed her eyes and willed herself not to think as she danced on with the crowd, her clothes growing sweaty, the beat of the music filling her head.

Yeah, she was all in.

She had to be. Really, there just was no other choice.

Chapter Seven

"I can't believe you made it!" Lizzy said, coming up behind Kate. Kate spun to look at her. She'd been discreetly tracking Lizzy's progress around the room since the band's final song ended, ten minutes earlier. Lizzy took the time to speak personally with all her customers, first one, then the next. All of them touched her arm or hugged her in reassurance. Kate sighed as she watched.

Mindy's planned sabotage of the garage was becoming a little too real.

At one point, Lizzy was talking to a small woman with spiky gray hair and a 35 mm camera around her neck. She was talking to Lizzy animatedly, as if wanting to make plans and organize, and Lizzy was nodding thoughtfully. Then suddenly, Lizzy looked up and smiled directly at Kate. A thrill traveled through Kate's body and she smiled back. Not unexpectedly, her heart began beating furiously once more.

Damn adrenaline, Kate thought as she tried to steady herself.

Now, Lizzy was finally standing right in front of her. "Your fans certainly love you, as well they should," she commented.

"Oh," Lizzy began, bashfully. "Well, we like to get in the groove, you know. It's R&B," she declared as if that explained the appeal.

"No, Lizzy, they love *you*," Kate emphasized. "And they love what you and Tenika do here. And, well, I love it, too," she said a little more fervently. *That was awkward,* she thought.

Kate paused, trying to get hold of herself. *Don't blow it,* her brain screamed silently.

"Anyway, I'm very sorry about your bad news," Kate said gently, her eyes trained on the floor as she did her best to feign innocence.

"Can't stop progress, I guess," said Lizzy. Taking a long breath, she folded her arms across her chest and glanced around. "It's going to be so weird not to have this place anymore." She looked back at Kate. "I mean, we've been here for years. I don't really know what life will be like without Driven."

They studied each other for a long moment, and Kate felt something simply give and open up inside her. There was connection there. Pure, simple, honest connection. "I'm sure," she practically whispered, unable to take her eyes off of Lizzy. Kate realized in that instant that she would go anywhere Lizzy told her to go. And she would do damn near anything that was asked of her.

Kate wasn't exactly sure why her feelings were so strong after such a short amount of time. She just knew there was something powerful here, and it was definitive.

"What are you doing right now?" Lizzy asked.

Kate looked around. "Oh, well, nothing," she said stiffly. "I should really get home, but…" Gazing into Lizzy's eyes was making it difficult to finish her sentence.

"Good," said Lizzy. "Don't leave. Let me help the band break stuff down, then let's have a beer together, okay?" She turned back. "Or a glass of wine? I think we have some chardonnay around here somewhere…" She held Kate's gaze. "Just don't go," she added.

"I won't," Kate immediately promised. "And I can help—" she began, but Lizzy brushed her off.

"You stay right there and relax," she said. "I'll be right back."

Kate liked the sound of that, she realized as she watched Lizzy walk away.

*

"You come sit over here," Tenika suggested, giving the chair by the cash register a pat. "Lizzy will be right along."

Kate followed and took her seat. "I think that's for you," Tenika said, motioning to the glass of chilled chardonnay that now rested on top of the appointment book.

"Oh, how lovely," Kate said as she picked up the wine glass and took a sip. Chilled wine seeped into her brain, instantly relaxing all her neurons and paving the way back to inner peace. They sat in tired silence for a moment. Then Tenika gave a yawn, picked up her messenger bag, slung it over her shoulder and turned to head for the door. "Have a good one," she called to Kate as she left.

Kate sat idly for a few more moments, waiting as the last of the band gear was packed into cars outside. There was no sign of Lizzy. As Kate sat there, she couldn't help but notice the appointment book for the garage, spread open before her.

Specifically, Kate noticed how few appointments were written on its pages. *This couldn't be all of them*, she thought miserably. But, of course, it probably was. Once more, Kate reminded herself this garage was about to go under.

Because of her boss.

And because of her.

Stop it! Kate commanded her brain. She took down the bad review on Yelp. It had only been up for 48 hours. She did what she could.

"Wow, what's the matter?" Lizzy asked from the doorway. She walked over to where Kate was sitting. Now the two of them were alone in the garage. "You look like you've got some serious shit going on."

"Oh, it's just work. Whatever, it's nothing," Kate said, quickly pasting a smile on her face.

"Where do you work again?" Lizzy asked, opening the mini fridge under the counter in search of a beer.

"An accounting firm," Kate lied. "Nothing exciting." *Jesus*, Kate thought to herself. *Accounting? Why was she lying like this to Lizzy?* But then what other options did she have?

"Huh," said Lizzy. "I would have pegged you as more of a creative type. Marketing or PR or art museums or something." She shut the door of the mini fridge with her foot and popped her beer open.

"Ah, well, I'm pretty boring as it turns out," Kate insisted.

Taking a long pull of her beer, Lizzy leaned back against the counter and studied Kate. "I'd hardly call you boring," she said. "In fact, you're one of the most interesting women I've met in a long time."

Kate blushed and looked down at her hands that were practically tying a Gordian Knot out of her fingers. There was a palpable silence between them.

Shaking her hands free, Kate smiled. Now there was an awkward pause. "I'm nervous," she finally admitted.

"Because of me?" Lizzy asked with a small smile.

Kate laughed and looked at the ceiling. "Yes, I suppose," she said. Then she returned her gaze to Lizzy.

"I don't mind that at all," Lizzy said. "You can be however you want to be."

God, this woman is smooth, Kate thought. But also, she was just plain sweet. She took a sip of her wine. "Grand," said Kate. Another silence ensued for a moment.

Suddenly it seemed as if there was both nothing and everything to talk about.

"Tell me about your work troubles," said Lizzy. "What's going on?"

"Oh, Jesus," muttered Kate. "I work for a psychopath. But let's not get into all that. Let's talk about you instead, shall we?"

"I'm good with psychopaths," Lizzy said. "My degree was in psychology."

"Not this one," murmured Kate. "She's..." Again, her voice disappeared. Suddenly, she turned to Lizzy, emboldened. "You know, you don't have to lose this place, Lizzy."

Lizzy's eyebrows shot up. "Oh? What makes you say that?"

"I wouldn't give up hope until they're padlocking the door," Kate asserted.

"Well, we're doing our best, but so far we got one oil change out of the gig tonight," she said with a sigh. "We're gonna need a lot more than that to stay open, Marta."

Kate's fake name hung in the air awkwardly between them. She really needed to do something about that, she realized.

But when?

Now?

"All you need is better marketing," Kate declared, moving on. "That's what will bring the customers in."

"Yeah, we thought of some sort of raffle or something, but, you know, this stuff is so not my deal." Lizzy shook her head. "I'm an idiot when it comes to marketing."

"You just need an event," said Kate, warming to the subject. "A sales event. And you need a contest with a really sexy prize. Something all the women want."

Lizzy just looked at her, rapt.

Kate continued, now hitting her stride. "So what do all the women who come to your garage want?" she asked rhetorically. "Besides work on their cars?"

"Love and sex?" Lizzy joked.

"Precisely!" Kate burst. "So have an automotive event that's all about love and sex."

Lizzy laughed out loud. "*What?*"

"Think about it, Lizzy," Kate continued. "Valentine's Day is almost here. It's a perfect opportunity. You should always try to connect things to public holidays if you can, brings in the media and such," she buzzed on. "Anyway everyone hates being alone on Valentine's Day, right? So I'm thinking love, romance, candlelit dinners. How about you give away a romantic dinner for two? But only IF they buy your—"

"Wait a minute, *what* are you suggesting?" Lizzy interjected, unable to contain herself.

The gleam of a good idea now took over Kate's entire being, and she drew herself up. "Valentine's Day lube jobs!" she announced triumphantly.

The two women looked at each other and burst out laughing. "Oh my God. That is *brilliant!*" Lizzy howled.

"I do actually think it's a good one," Kate agreed modestly.

Grabbing her phone, Lizzy punched the autodial for Tenika. She put the call on speaker.

"Our problems are solved," Lizzy began as Tenika picked up the phone.

"Lizzy! I'm trying to go to bed over here," Tenika's voice said with a trace of annoyance.

"No, T! Listen up! I'm talking to Marta, and she's got an amazing idea for us," Lizzy crowed. "Tell her, Marta!"

"Hi, Tenika," Kate said into the phone. "Not to keep you awake, but what about a special on Valentine's Day lube jobs and a contest giving away a romantic dinner for two? Only the first 50 or 100 who book and buy get in. Keep it limited. A five day sale that starts in just a few days…in time for the holiday."

Lizzy picked up the phone, and pulled it closer. "How many lube jobs can we do in a week?" she asked Tenika.

"Oh, we'll do 100 if we have to," Tenika said. "I'm in."

"Thought you'd be," remarked Lizzy.

"Nice work, Marta," Tenika added. "*Valentine's Day lube jobs…*" they heard her telling Delilah as she hung up. Lizzy put the phone back in her pocket with a smile.

"You can call it 'Find Love at Driven Garage' and target all the lesbian listservs in the area," Kate continued. "Put a reasonable price on it, then get a local nice restaurant to sponsor the evening for two so the prize is free. Get a limo for the night, and get a florist in on it, also free. They love this kind of exposure."

Lizzy looked at Kate. "You know, Marta," she said. "You are seriously good at this. Are you sure you've never done this before?"

Kate blushed. "Oh, it's just a few ideas," she said modestly.

"I mean, you could do this professionally," Lizzy said, shaking her head in amazement.

Stop now, Kate cautioned herself. *Either stop or tell this poor woman the truth about who you are.* Kate knew that if there was ever a moment to come clean, this surely was it.

Still, she hesitated, and said nothing. She couldn't tell Lizzy. Not now. Not yet.

For one brief night in her life, Kate just needed to just be in the thrall of new love, unimpeded. It was such an unfamiliar, tender and pure experience, she simply couldn't bear to let it go. Even if she had to keep a lie going.

Kate stood up, trying to ignore the aching finality of her lie. And folding her arms, she walked through the garage casting an appraising eye around her. Lizzy followed in her wake. "You know, it wouldn't take much to clean this place up, and I think it would make a big difference," she noted. "Auto garages run by men tend to be grimy, but women prefer a place that's tidy, nicely lit and painted. Clean. Have you thought about repainting? Perhaps fixing it up a bit?"

"Yeah, we talked about that, but we have, like, no time," Lizzy admitted. "Or at least we didn't. But I guess we do now, so tell me what you're thinking."

Kate walked over to a corner stacked high with auto part boxes. Then she turned to Lizzy. "Do you have another space to store these?" she asked.

"We have some odd space in the back room. More if we clean it out."

"If you did that, you could paint this corner of the garage …" Kate began as she mused aloud. Suddenly she turned to Lizzy. "How many of those Valentine's Day lube jobs could you do per hour?"

"With the two of us working, at least four. Maybe six?" Lizzy replied.

"And what's your profit?"

"We could make maybe 20 or 30 dollars on each, depending on the oil we use."

"So that's roughly three to four thousand dollars a week," Kate continued. "But, Lizzy, that's only the half of it. Because you can do much more for them than just lube jobs, correct? And that is where the sustainable business model lives."

"Explain," said Lizzy, not quite following.

"Once you fill up that roster with lube jobs, then you get your customers to stay here, waiting for their cars," Kate's eyes lit up with possibility. "I'm thinking you add a comfortable couch right in this corner. You want to encourage a bit of conversation, so make this corner cozy. Paint it a pretty color, put in a lovely table and chairs, some softer lighting. You set out a jigsaw puzzle, a few card games and the like. Tea and coffee, of course," she continued. "You do whatever it takes to get the women in here. Because once you get them to start talking…really anything could happen," she said, looking directly at Lizzy.

"Huh," said Lizzy, pondering the plan. "So Driven becomes a place for hook ups?"

"Or finding a partner," Kate said modestly.

Lizzy looked up at Kate in wonder. Then she shook her head. "Are you sure this will work? *Here?*"

Kate nodded. "I do. Anyway, you have nothing to lose," she said. "So what do you think?"

Lizzy looked at her and smiled broadly. "I think I wish I'd met you sooner," she replied.

*

An hour and a half later, the ad was written and posted to lesbian listservs and meet-ups throughout the East Bay. Kate even created a coupon that Lizzy could distribute as a flyer to promote the event.

"How do you know all this stuff?" Lizzy kept asking as she watched Kate whiz along on her computer, typing and tapping.

"Just do," she said vaguely. Finally, she looked up at Lizzy. "Where's that glass of wine?" she asked.

Lizzy topped off her glass of chardonnay and handed it to her. Kate took a long sip. It was past midnight now, and her brain was completely fried. Still, the wine had a rejuvenating effect. This was her brain on adrenaline, creativity and lust.

"Don't forget to call that restaurant owner you know first thing tomorrow," she said. "And a florist, too. You'll want a nice arrangement for your new conversation corner, and one for the winners. I think there's a new florist over on College Avenue, over by the Rockridge Cafe. They'd be likely to want to drum up business and give you a sponsorship. And maybe they'd put out tent cards on the tables for the promotion."

Lizzy was starting to sag visibly in front of her. Kate knew she needed to slow down. "Oh, dear. Have I worn you out?" she asked with a laugh.

"Uh, yeah," admitted Lizzy. "But it's a good worn out! I mean, I'm incredibly grateful and excited! And, sure, I'll call whoever you think I should call."

"All right then," Kate said as she rose from the desk. *This is it*, she thought to herself. Now was the moment she should succumb completely to Lizzy's charms, tell her who she is and see if there is even still a shadow of a chance with her.

Or, she could just walk away, knowing she'd done what she could for Lizzy. Perhaps she'd even managed to correct her catastrophic karma.

Kate realized, of course, that she was choosing the latter. There wasn't even a question. For one thing, she didn't have the nerve to tell Lizzy who she was. That would ultimately mean nothing less than quitting her job and taking a headlong dive into love.

No, Kate was going to do what Kate always did at such times. She was going to hunker down and self-protect.

Which meant she was going to walk away.

"Here," said Lizzy, grabbing her jacket from a hook on the wall. "I'll walk you out. I need to get home myself."

Kate watched silently as Lizzy moved around the space, turning off the lights and closing up. An ache had begun in her gut. It was the old loneliness. Kate took a deep breath and fought it back.

"Have I given you too much to do, cleaning up the place and such?" she asked, eager to move on to another thought.

"Hell, no! It's high time. T's been on me to do this for a couple of years. She's going to be thrilled. If I can get her to help me this weekend, we'll bang it out. Drink some coffee. Crank some music. Git 'er done."

Lizzy snapped off the last of the lights by the front door beside them, and together they stepped outside. She was wearing a faded honey-colored Carhartt jacket, and as the pink light of the buzzing street light cascaded over them, Kate's heart did a small flip. She watched Lizzy lower the huge corrugated doors over the open car bays with an accustomed grace and ease. To Kate, Lizzy seemed hotter than ever.

"Anyway," she said, pausing in front of Kate. "I'd like to take you to dinner some time. I mean, I owe you, Marta."

"Hush! You don't owe me a thing, Lizzy," Kate said. "I wanted to help you. "It's the right thing to do."

"What do you mean?" Lizzy asked. She looked at Kate curiously, and suddenly Kate felt vulnerable. A small stab of fear passed through her. Perhaps Lizzy was actually on to her. Her brain went into a microfreeze. This was why she didn't like to tell lies. Because in the end, they always caught up with you.

"I really have to go," she said, feeling the tension of the moment escalate as the two of them stood under the pink, buzzing street light. They were completely alone together on San Pablo Avenue. Finally, Kate turned away, but Lizzy pulled her back to face her again.

For a fleeting moment, Kate thought Lizzy might kiss her. But instead, there was a look of concern on Lizzy's face.

"What did you mean?" she asked again. "When you said helping me was the right thing to do?"

Backpedal. Backpedal NOW, Kate commanded herself.

"Anyone would help you, of course. That's all I'm saying" Kate insisted, "It's the decent thing to do and how humans need to treat each other. Cruelty and competition be damned, and all that. Right?"

"Oh," Lizzy said with a smile. "Okay." Still, her hand remained on Kate's arm. Slowly, almost reluctantly, she removed it.

They looked at each other one more time, and one more time Kate felt herself give way to the very essence of Lizzy. One more look passed between them, a long sip from their shared cup.

Kate wondered helplessly, *When will there ever be another like Lizzy?*

For a moment, she hesitated. Should she just go ahead and take a chance by telling Lizzy the truth? The question was a tantalizing one, hanging in front of her like ripe fruit.

"Guess we'd better go," Lizzy finally said.

"Yes! Yes," Kate agreed. "I just—"

Just what? I can't go because I'm completely fascinated by you?

"I wish you the very best of luck, Lizzy. I really do," Kate concluded a bit formally. "I truly wish I could help you more."

Oh, how she didn't want to go home. Not ever again, really.

"Well, hell. Come by tomorrow and we'll put you to work!" Lizzy crowed. "I've got plenty of paint rollers." But then she laughed. "I'm only kidding, Marta. Believe me, you've helped me plenty. You're amazing," she concluded more gently. "Can I walk you to your car?"

"It's right here," Kate said, pointing to her vehicle.

"Oh! Yeah, look at that," Lizzy said, and they both chuckled. "Well, have a good night." Lizzy looked at Kate one more time.

"Yeah, have a good night," Kate whispered.

So much was unsaid in those two simple phrases. Kate turned her back to Lizzy and shut her eyes, as a random tear escaped and slid down her cheek. Kate opened the car door and got in. Then she lowered the window. "Bye, Lizzy!" she called in as crisp a voice as she could command.

"See ya," Lizzy said as she turned and began to walk up the street. Kate watched her go in her rearview mirror, a lone backpack-clad figure disappearing into the night.

As if she could read Kate's mind, Lizzy suddenly turned around and stopped. "I'm going to see you again!" she called down the street. "I can feel it!"

Kate said nothing. Instead, she willed herself to start her engine and pull out of her spot. *Do not succumb. Do not go after her. Do not lose control in this singular, precious moment. Do not even think of telling her who you are. You need to keep it together.*

Drive away now, she commanded herself as the wheels turned and the car pulled out on to San Pablo. Once more, she looked back at Lizzy in her mirror.

Lizzy was standing there on the sidewalk, watching her go.

Damn, she thought.

Dammit to hell.

Chapter Eight

Tenika pulled out her key and inserted it into the padlock on the Driven gate. Giving it a crisp turn, she released the lock, yanked it out of its coupling, and pulled up the gate. Sunlight spilled into the garage where dozens of parts boxes were strewn all over the floor. In the midst of the pile, Lizzy was sitting cross-legged.

She peered up at Tenika, blinked and smiled. "Hey," she said softly.

Tenika studied her business partner for a moment, with her hands on her hips. "What the hell?" she said.

"I know it's a mess, but it's a beautiful mess, T," Lizzy said with excitement. "You're going to love this! We're doing a massive cleanup today. The whole garage, starting with the parts. Turns out you were totally right about that."

Tenika shook her head. "You get laid last night or something?"

"Ha, ha," Lizzy muttered a little indignantly. "I just got the rest of Marta's ideas. She was here past midnight, and I'm telling you, that woman is seriously good at this. She's like a marketing genius!" Jubilantly, Lizzy pulled a creased piece of paper from the pocket of her coveralls and waved it in Tenika's direction. "Take a look at this."

She handed over the sheet of marketing instructions, and Tenika began to study it. "Finding sponsors, setting up Facebook ads, passing out coupons at the lesbian bar... Seriously?" Tenika looked at Lizzy with mild panic. "This is like a whole marketing proposal."

"I know, it's incredible, isn't it?" Lizzy waxed on enthusiastically.

"But who's going to do all this stuff?" Tenika protested, putting her bag down on the floor. "And *when?* We've got less than no time."

Lizzy carried on, nonplussed. "I'm telling you, Marta's like a professional marketing consultant or something. Only she's not. She's an accountant, believe it or not."

"That's what she told you?" Tenika asked, her voice rising. "She told you she's an *accountant?* Lizzy, you've got to wake up, girl." Tenika's voice dropped down into a warning. "Let's not forget this person is using a fake name, and now she wants to redo our marketing. I don't know about this. I don't know about this at all," she cautioned.

"Who cares what she does for a living, T?" Lizzy protested. "Marta is saving our asses right now. Not to mention the fact that she's super-smart, kind-hearted, sensitive, gorgeous *and* has an incredibly cute accent not to mention great legs."

"I don't like it one bit," Tenika said.

"But I love it. And you said we need a big idea. So here it is! And get this! Marta wants us to store all the parts in the back room, then redo that corner so customers can sit around and pick each other up. We call it a conversation corner, and all the avail—"

"Wait a minute, *what are you saying?*" Tenika said, mildly offended. "Driven's going to turn into some pick up joint?"

"Yes!" Lizzy answered happily. "And here's the best part. You know how the lesbian bars never stay open? But every last one of those lesbians has a car. And they all need an oil change, right? So we just make a nice, cozy corner for them to chat each other up while we're servicing the vehicles. They come rolling on in here, find love and Driven gets a whole new life!"

Tenika stood back and looked at her partner. Then she sighed and handed back the sheet of paper. "Baby girl, you've gotta get a grip."

"What?" Lizzy said innocently. Standing up, she dusted off her hands. "All we have to do is stash the parts, repaint that corner, bring in some nice furniture, buy a better coffeemaker and call some florists, and shit like that."

"I know! I know. I read the document, Lizzy," Tenika's exasperation was apparent. "Listen, just because you're falling in love doesn't mean this is a good idea."

Lizzy blushed now. "Is it really that obvious?" she asked in a low voice.

"Totally," Tenika said.

"Well, hell. Don't worry about it, T, because I've gotten nowhere with her anyway. But…she sure is cute."

"You mean you're not dating already?"

Lizzy looked down at the floor of the garage. "I have no idea if she even likes me," she admitted. "It feels like she does, but she keeps retreating."

Tenika folded her arms and looked at her best friend. She hadn't seen Lizzy this awake, alive or even this perplexed in ages. What she'd seen was Lizzy in a gray funk for the past year. But now, apparently, all that gloom was over. Tenika was silent.

"Anyway," Lizzy continued. "If there's something there, she'll be back. And if there isn't, well, then I guess I was wrong."

Tenika cleared her throat. "I'm glad your heart and your yaya are back online, Lizzy. I really am. But we have a business to run and—"

"But you said yourself, T, that her ideas were good."

"They *are* good," Tenika admitted. "I'm just saying they may be a little too good. What if she works for that other garage, the one that's trying to drive us out of business? What if this is some kind of a set up?"

"T, I seriously doubt that. I mean, why would she give us good ideas?" Lizzy asked. "Wouldn't she give us terrible ideas if she was trying to hurt the business?"

To this, Tenika had no answer. "I haven't got a clue," she admitted. Then she picked up her bag and headed over to the coffeemaker, making her way through the boxed auto parts on the floor.

She stopped and looked at Lizzy. "You sure you're okay?" Tenika pressed. "You didn't sleep with her or anything, right? I just don't want to see you get your heart broken."

"I can take care of myself," Lizzy gently reminded her.

"Most of the time you can, anyway," Tenika remarked. Then looking back at her partner, she softened slightly and gave a small sigh. "Okay, then," she agreed. "I guess we really are doing a make-over," she chuckled. "All it took was damn near shutting down."

"This is progress!" Lizzy burst. "100% progress!"

Tenika smiled to herself. Lizzy was, indeed, back.

*

Kate peered into her open laptop on the kitchen table as she stirred her coffee. The first announcement for the Valentine's Day lube jobs had just dropped. "Find Love at Driven Garage!" trumpeted the headline in the email newsletter.

Mindy came into the kitchen and peered over Kate's shoulder. "What's that?" she asked. Then she peered closer and read the ad. "Give me a break!" she sniffed in response.

Kate started to close her laptop, but Mindy's hand closed on her shoulder. "Wait," she said. "I want to read the entire thing." Kate closed her eyes. Mindy's hand on her shoulder felt like a forty-pound vice clamping down on her.

Mindy was silent for a moment more as she read the ad once more. "Are they kidding?" she howled. "Stupid doesn't even begin to describe this."

"I thought it was a pretty good idea, actually," Kate volunteered. Mindy shot her a look as she pulled open the refrigerator and extracted a massive bag of baby kale.

"Sure, if you want to be the desperate garage that will try anything to stay in business," Mindy countered. "Then it's totally the way to go. But any way, like I said, they're desperate. They need to flail before they die."

Mindy jammed the blender full of kale, threw in some frozen bananas, a shot of protein powder, and some coconut water. Then she turned it on to full speed. The roar of the Vitamix filled the kitchen.

"I'd say they aren't dead yet," Kate observed.

"What?" Mindy yelled over the din of the machine.

"Nothing," Kate countered. She needed to say as little as possible at this moment, because imminent love was still pulsing through her body. She hadn't slept more than a few hours, and her entire nervous system felt like it had been hijacked by her encounter with Lizzy.

Ever since she'd woken up, it had been *Lizzy, Lizzy, Lizzy* in a nonstop loop through Kate's brain.

Now Kate began to fake a few coughs. "You know," she said, still hacking mildly. "I'm really not feeling very well today."

Mindy said nothing. Instead, she reached for a glass and poured herself a smoothie the color of green vomit. "There's a lot to do today, Kate. For starters, there's the visa situation. That's not resolved yet..." she began.

But instead of listening as Mindy droned on, Kate got up, closed her laptop and left the room. Still doing her best to cough convincingly, she climbed the stairs back to her room. Then she lay down in her bed once more.

Kate was far from ill. Instead, she was awash in delight. She was filled with gladness. She wanted to sing loudly. To stretch in the sun. To pour her heart out in an endless string of bad poetry.

Kate was feverish, all right. But it was the kind of feverish that came with the confirmation of love.

She knew now, without a doubt, that Lizzy wanted her. Lizzy hadn't been shy about it, not at all. In fact, she'd been downright flirtatious. Meanwhile, Lizzy fulfilled every last requirement Kate had in mind for the official love of her life.

The list of her excellent qualifications ran through Kate's mind. Lizzy was strong, sympathetic, caring, powerful, empathetic, curious, a good listener, cute, funny, charming...and hot.

No, Kate knew that there was no way in hell that she could go into her job today, put on the mask and assume the position of a loyal supplicant to her boss, her housemate. Her captor.

She walked over to the bedroom door and opened it cautiously. She could hear Mindy still moving around the kitchen. "Mindy?" she called.

"What?" As usual, Mindy's voice was tinged with annoyance.

"I'm..." Kate coughed, for effect. "I'm not going to make it in today, I'm afraid. Think I'm running a fever."

She heard Mindy swear under her breath. "Kate, I'm leaving for my retreat in three hours!" she yelled back. "Someone has to be at the garage, someone has to... Oh, *screw it*," she cried in frustration. "Fine! Stay home," she spat. Then her tone grew icier. "Do you think you can still manage to take care of the dog while I'm gone?"

"Of course," Kate coughed.

A moment later, Kate heard the wheels of Mindy's suitcase click across the kitchen floor.

Then the back door shut, and Mindy's car started up. Kate listened to her drive away.

The deed was done. Mindy would be gone for a glorious three days.

Giving a sigh of relief, Kate shut her bedroom door and retreated back to bed. She was on her own. At least for today.

*

Nearly four hours passed, and Kate was still in her pajamas pouring over her laptop. Mr. Big lay snoring softly in the corner, and filtered sunlight painted broad stripes across her bed, warming her sanctuary.

Kate was miles away at the moment. Specifically, she was reading USA.gov yet again to determine what it would take to finally get a green card so she could have some kind of legal status in The States. A green card always seemed just out of reach the entire time she'd worked for Mindy.

Kate paused at the section titled "Reporting an Immigration Violation." This was, of course, the biggest risk of leaving her job. Nothing would stop Mindy from picking up the phone and calling ICE agents on Kate.

Skipping over it, Kate clicked on the section titled, "How to Become a U.S. Citizen." She read and then re-read the same section she'd studied over the years. As always, she paid special attention to the line, "You may be eligible to apply as an immigrant worker."

Kate didn't qualify for any of the special case exemptions. She wasn't an Indo-Chinese citizen who'd emigrated before 1979. Nor was she a human-trafficking victim, or even an American Indian born in Canada. No, she was just an Irish girl who'd come to the U.S. on vacation and never went home. Which was the very worst way to arrive in the U.S. if you wanted a green card.

Closing the laptop with a snap, Kate lay back in the pillows and considered her fate. She had to quit her job, that much she knew. Not only was it obvious that Mindy would do nothing to actually help her get the much-needed green card, her job was quietly killing her spirit every day. She also realized the effect her work had on the people Mindy targeted, specifically her new best friends, Lizzy and Tenika.

Kate was simply at one of those crossroads in life where she had to act. She couldn't avoid or endlessly debate the decision one minute longer. Lizzy or no Lizzy, she needed to quit her job, and make her own way in the world. Even if it meant returning to her small seaside hamlet near Dublin.

Back in the day, she had been afraid to come out. She'd had one brief, furtive affair in Ireland, with the butch who was her lab partner in university chemistry. It had been just enough to confirm that, yes, she was indeed gay. And it had quickly crumbled once her parents started asking questions about what 'lad' they assumed she was busy with until the wee hours.

At the time, Kate had no answer for them. She dared not tell them the truth. But, as one would expect, they found out. She and Sinead had been spotted at a pub two towns over. All they'd been doing was lifting a pint, but of course there was hell to pay. The fact that Sinead was such an obvious butch made it clear what was going on.

Kate had not been back to the 'new' gay-friendly Ireland since she'd left for California.

She'd find a completely changed place if she got deported. Her sister had told her all about it. These days, there were even transgender rights and legalized same-sex marriage. There might even be a thriving lesbian community in the city by now.

Kate tried to feel optimistic as she gazed out of her bedroom window.

Her own parents, of course, were the real problem. No matter what went on in Ireland, they were still hopeless homophobes. They were old-school Catholics who considered homosexuality nothing less than an abomination. They could make her reentry into Ireland a living hell.

Yet again, Kate could feel the familiar ache in her soul. The endless shaming. The permanent lack of approval. The bleak, sad feeling that she was a problem, no matter what she did. Or who she was, or what she thought, or who she loved, or even where she lived. Going home to Ireland meant being in striking distance of her parents once again. And the prospect filled her with a steady, quiet dread.

No matter what she did, the response would be the same. "Suit yourself," her mother would rebuke "You always do anyway."

Yes, she was getting ahead of herself. She had to consider all the options. Perhaps she could keep her job just long enough to find a cheap lawyer and actually get a green card. Of course, that could take another few years. Maybe ten.

Kate sighed in despair.

Waiting that long really would kill her.

She could try to find a fake husband, some nice gay man who needed to be married to a woman for his own reasons. But, the days of hiding sexual identity were pretty much over. These days, what self-respecting gay man wouldn't want to marry someone he actually loved? This entire green card model simply didn't work anymore.

The other option was hanging on to her job until she found a wife.

Maybe Lizzy was a suitable candidate.

Oh for God's sake! She'd just met the woman. Furthermore, she had no idea if they could even have a peaceful relationship, if they were even a match. Kate didn't even know Lizzy. In this terrible and scary moment, she was nothing more than a beautiful, convenient fantasy.

It was really best to pretend this option didn't even exist, Kate reminded herself. She needed to focus on staying beneath the radar and finding a better job. And if all of it ended, and she got deported, then so be it.

Truthfully, in this time and place, Kate had little control. This was simply how it was.

At least she'd had the chance to live in the U.S. as long as she did. She'd met Lizzy. And now she'd finally found the courage to leave Mindy's company and forge her own path. These were not small accomplishments, and Kate was truly grateful for them.

Now the only question was how to quit. And when.

Kate sat up in the sunlight, gave a long stretch and stood up. She looked at Mr. Big glumly regarding her from the floor.

"Go for a walk?" she asked.

The dog looked at her warily as if he didn't quite believer her.

"At the very least, *I* need a walk," she told the dog as she peeled off her pajamas. "I need a walk and considerably more."

Looking in the mirror, Kate smiled at herself. She would leave her job. She would do this because she could do it and because she needed to. Never mind the cascade of flutters that began in her sternum and moved down through her belly every time she thought about quitting.

Still, Kate had a ready defense. Just the mere thought of Lizzy, or even of Lizzy and her together, would power her through every last concern.

Humming, Kate turned on the shower and stepped in.

It might actually be a decent day after all.

*

Kate sat in traffic one mile from Driven Garage and looked at her phone. Mindy was calling again, presumably from the Denver airport. But instead of answering, she turned off the ringer and tossed the phone in her bag.

She'd walked the dog, rewrote her resume and even packed a small suitcase. It was just enough to get her settled in another place, though exactly where remained to be seen. She'd even combed the web and looked for a new place to live. The initial forays into East Bay apartment listings had been immediately depressing.

There was nothing she could afford out here, nothing at all. But that was just today, she told herself. Anything could happen tomorrow.

It was strictly one day at a time with her new half-plan. Kate would go with the flow as she went. And if she had to take it one hour, or even one minute at a time, that's what she would do.

All Kate knew at this moment was that her heart and her soul were driving her across town, demanding that she see Lizzy again. Maybe she could help her and Tenika fix up the garage. After all, Lizzy had invited her to help, hadn't she?

Nervously, Kate glanced at the dashboard clock once more. It was well past five, and Lizzy would undoubtedly be getting out of work soon. Kate hoped she hadn't already missed her. The light changed to green, and Kate stepped on the gas.

Suddenly a pang of doubt came over her. What if she'd misinterpreted Lizzy's compliments? What if Lizzy wasn't really interested in her at all?

What if Lizzy was just friendly like this with everyone?

What if she was about to completely embarrass herself?

But then there was an even more terrifying thought. What if Kate actually told Lizzy who she really was and Lizzy felt so angry and betrayed she decided never to speak to her again?

Kate swallowed hard as tears sprang into her eyes. In this moment, she felt so alone and so vulnerable, it was all she could do to stay focused and simply drive. Mostly, she knew she needed to stop lying to Lizzy, no matter what her response. That lie, alone, was seriously unhinging her.

Breathe, breathe, she commanded herself. *Just show up and say hello. No harm in that.*

Job or no job, Kate knew what she had to do.

A few moments later, Kate pulled up outside of Driven and got out of her car. She could see Lizzy at work alone in the shadows of the garage. It appeared that Tenika was gone. Her feet felt unsteady on the sidewalk as she approached.

Taking a deep breath, Kate squared her shoulders. "Hi, Lizzy," she called.

Lizzy looked up and immediately happy surprise filled her face. "Hey!" she called out, putting down the wrench in her hands. She pulled a rag from her pocket and wiped her hands. "I said I was going to see you again!" she said as she strode toward Kate.

"Oh, I was just, you know, being a good neighbor and such," Kate said. She realized she was making no sense, but Lizzy didn't appear to care. She just stood there, hands on her hips, beaming at Kate. Kate, meanwhile, was trying to stay calm despite a heart that was nearly beating out of her chest.

"I'm seriously glad you made it back here," Lizzy said. "I'm just finishing up. Have a beer with me?"

"Oh, no, I'm on my way to do some things," Kate hedged.

Instantly, her mind sputtered and fumed. *What are you doing? This is exactly what you wanted!*

Kate could feel herself shaking slightly as she stood there, delivering her offer to Lizzy. "I thought I'd just, uh, volunteer to help," she said. "If you need another painter, that is. Or help you pick out some furniture for the remodel. Or anything, really," she said, her eyes moving rapidly around the garage.

Kate's voice trailed off, and she looked at Lizzy.

"Really? You'd do that?" Lizzy asked. She seemed amazed.

"Of course," Kate said, melting into her gaze. "You asked me to come help."

"Oh, I was kidding! I mean, no obligation, Marta," Lizzy insisted. Now she seemed embarrassed.

A sudden calm descended over Kate. "I want to help you," she said genuinely.

Lizzy seemed to lean in her direction. "And we would love your help. Like seriously, Marta." Lizzy motioned over to the former parts corner, which was now empty of everything but for several gallons of paint and some rollers. "We followed your suggestions and we're all ready to go! Hey, did you see the ad? It seems to be all over the place. This is going to be amazing!"

"I did see it," said Kate. "It looks great."

The two women looked at each other, and there it was again. Pure quicksilver connection. Heart on heart, eyes locked. This time Kate felt it ricochet through her body and descend straight into her groin.

"Yeah," said Lizzy. Awkwardly she took out the rag and wiped her hands. "I just—" she began.

"Yes?" Kate interrupted.

They both stopped and smiled at each other.

Lizzy continued. "I was going to text you, but I don't have your number."

Nor do you even know who I am, Kate thought. Was she actually going to give her cell phone number to this woman she wanted with every fiber of her being, even though she was so very dangerous to her entire existence?

Kate was silent. It felt like a moment of truth. Was this the moment to tell Lizzy who she actually was? It would make everything so clear and simple, for once in her life.

Then she'd know. Lizzy would either be on board, or she wouldn't. So another piece of Kate's future could fall neatly into place.

Or not.

Yet again, Kate hesitated. She opened her mouth to respond, fully expecting to tell Lizzy who she was. Instead, she heard herself dutifully recite her phone number.

Coolly, Lizzy pulled her phone from her pocket, and typed in the information. Then she looked up and smiled at her. "Sure you don't want that beer? Or wait—I still have that bottle of chardonnay."

Kate felt something loosen up and give. "Well, alright," she said slowly. "Maybe a quick chardonnay."

Lizzy shrugged as she headed off to the mini fridge. "Never know," she smiled over her shoulder. "Could be a slow one." She poured the glass of wine and handed it to Kate. Then she lifted her glass.

"To reinvention," she said. The two of them touched glasses.

You don't know the half of it, thought Kate, taking a cold, dry sip of the wine. She lowered her head for a moment, as if letting her thoughts collect. Then she looked up at Lizzy. "I want to thank you," she said.

Lizzy looked surprised. "What did I do?"

Feeling emboldened, Kate took another long sip. Liquid courage was already having its effect. "Inviting me to help," she explained. "I needed that."

"Oh?" Lizzy replied.

"Work. Stress. Troubles," Kate said vaguely. "Right now I need some fun in my life."

Lizzy chuckled. "Well, Marta, that I can provide."

Marta. The fake name invaded their shared moment like a bad seed. *She'd get to that when she was ready. But not yet.*

They drank together in silence for one more moment. Kate found herself oddly tongue-tied, and she looked at Lizzy. Lizzy had grown quiet as well.

"Have you been in the U.S. a long time?" Lizzy asked to break the silence.

"Seven years. I feel more Californian than Irish at this point."

"Must be hard, living far away from home," Lizzy remarked.

"I suppose," offered Kate. "Unless you're in the place where you belong."

Again they fell silent. Suddenly, Kate felt hugely vulnerable. She pulled her sweater a little more tightly around her. "Anyway …" she said, a propos of nothing.

"Yeah," said Lizzy, looking into her eyes a little more deeply. "Anyway."

Lizzy cleared her throat, and Kate took a sip of wine. Then Kate suddenly stood up. "I'm afraid I have things to get to," she said, abandoning her half-finished glass of wine. "But this has been lovely."

"Oh, okay," Lizzy said.

"Lovely to talk," volunteered Kate.

"Yeah. It was," Lizzy said slowly, still looking her in the eye. "Do you still want to come paint tomorrow?"

"I do," Kate said.

"Come in the morning then. I'll have the coffee on by eight."

Kate smiled at Lizzy. "I'll be here, ready to paint," she affirmed.

Lizzy nodded and smiled. "I'll text you if anything changes."

"Please do," Kate said. *Please text me. Please, please, please.*

"Bye," she said.

"Bye," Lizzy said.

Finally, Kate turned away and got back into her car. Starting the engine, she started straight ahead.

What on earth had she just done?

Chapter Nine

"And how can I help you, miss?" asked the aging African American man behind the counter. A yellow bandanna covered his graying hair, and he wore the bakery's signature flour-dusted white apron.

Kate produced a paper bag filled with Arizmendi's still-warm cinnamon rolls, and he peered inside. The worker-owned co-op, something of an East Bay institution, was filled to the brim on Saturday morning with a line out the door. Mothers with strollers, sweaty post-run joggers and aging African grannies in white linen, their shawls draped over their heads, all waited patiently for their turn.

"Half dozen?" he asked.

"About that, I'd say," she confirmed.

"We'll call it good," he said casually as he punched her order into the cash register.

Kate was coming to Driven laden with carbs and sugar. And not just any. They were arguably the East Bay's finest carbs and sugar. Kate figured this would help when she finally had to deliver the truth that had been keeping her up all night.

Today was, indeed, the day of truth. Kate promised herself that by the time she went to bed tonight, Lizzy would know exactly who she was. And she would know just where they stood with each other.

This was the one uncertainty in her life that was firmly in Kate's control. Furthermore, she was done being a liar. It chafed at her soul.

"Thanks, have a lovely day," Kate said, taking the bag of cinnamon rolls and tucking them under her arm. She dropped a dollar in the jar collecting money for the local food bank. Then she untied Mr. Big from a nearby lamppost and proceeded down the street to The Canine Sanctuary, Mindy's preferred boarding place for Mr. Big.

She couldn't wait to get the snuffling little beast off her hands and get on with her own life.

*

"You are *seriously* turning in to a morning person, that's for damn sure," Tenika exclaimed. She studied her business partner. "I mean, it's not even eight on a Saturday morning. What's got into you, girl? That's two days in a row!"

"Hey, T!" Lizzy called, looking up from the five-gallon vat of off-white paint she was stirring. "I've been here since 6:30, but I didn't want to start without you," she admitted.

"Come *on!*"

"Yep," Lizzy said. "No lie. I've got it bad."

"I feel it," commented Tenika.

Lizzy put down the stirring rod and shook her head. "T, I haven't slept for two days. And that was when I thought I'd never see her again. I'm just, I don't know…"

"Lost in a cloud of lust," Tenika observed. "Too bad she disappeared on you."

"Actually, now that you mention it…" Lizzy began, focusing squarely on pouring the open bucket of paint in front of her into a rolling tray. She was uncertain how T would respond to her next piece of news.

"Now what?" sighed her business partner. Tenika folded her arms with a look of grim determination. "What's up, Lizzy?"

Lizzy could barely glance at her. "Marta showed up here last night."

"'Marta,'" T said, making little air quotations with her fingers.

"Anyway, she'll be here any minute. She wants to help us today."

"She's coming *here?* Now?" Tenika's voice gave a little squeak.

"Yep. I'm sorry I didn't check with you," Lizzy looked at her like a lost puppy. "I figured many hands make light work. And you seemed to be less suspicious of her the last time we talked. Anyway…"

"Hello!" called Kate gaily from the doorway. "Breakfast has arrived!"

Tenika rolled her eyes and shook her head at Lizzy. Then she turned around to greet their visitor. "Marta," she said, extending her hand. "Come on in."

"Thanks for including me," said Kate, shaking Tenika's outstretched hand. "Point me to the rollers. And, here," She handed her offering to Tenika. "Cinnamon rolls from Arizmendi."

Tenika chuckled and glanced at Lizzy. "Not everyone arrives with Arizmendi pastries," she remarked dryly, heading off toward the coffeemaker.

"Hi, there," Kate said to Lizzy, who was still standing over the paint. "Nice color," she observed.

Lizzy smiled up at her. "Hi," she said as a bit of pink rose up in her face. She glanced up at Kate shyly. "I'm glad you like it. Decorating isn't really in my wheelhouse. It's called Mountain Mushroom."

"It's a nice, clean color. It's all about what you do with the space, you know."

"Is it?" asked Lizzy a little dreamily.

"It is," affirmed Kate as they smiled at each other for a moment.

"Alright then," said Lizzy, pulling the rollers from their plastic packaging. "Who's ready to roll?"

*

Two hours later, the client conversation corner had a base coat, and now Lizzy, Tenika and Kate were taking a break outside in the sun. "I like rolling paint," Kate commented. "It's actually quite calming."

"Isn't it?" said Lizzy.

"I just like cutting in the edge," said Tenika. "Rolling is just one big paint spray. I mean, look at me." She held her arm out so the two could see the beige paint speckles. Kate laughed.

"Yeah, you do seem to be wearing a fine coating of Mountain Mushroom. Take my paintbrush," she volunteered. "I don't mind rolling at all."

They'd spent the morning making small talk as they'd painted. Kate filled them in on growing up in a pub in Ireland, and the fine points of ordering various Guinness drinks. "You never, ever want to order a Black and Tan," Kate cautioned. "That takes people back to the military police and the troubles, and no one wants to go there. Better to order a Black and Black so your stout comes with a shot of black currant."

In turn, Tenika shared what it was like growing up in Oakland. "None of this was here," Tenika said, waving her arm out. "That slick brewpub up the street with the ten-dollar beers? That was a plain old mom and pop deli called Serv-Rite. They sold Red Hots. We all went in there when we were hungry. The owner used to just give them to us. It was community, you know?"

Lizzy was stretched out on the bench beside the other two, her eyes closed happily beneath the heat of the sun. Opening her eyes, she glanced over at Kate contentedly. "So how'd you get a name like Marta, anyway? That's not Irish, is it?"

For a moment, Kate froze. She'd only been there for two hours. It was most certainly not time yet to divulge her story. *This was what happens when I let my guard down,* she worried.

"Oh, you know," she flummoxed. "The Black Irish and all that." She had no idea where she was going with this.

Lizzy looked at her. "Black Irish?"

"Invaders centuries ago. Celts, maybe. Really, who knows?" hedged Kate, hoping ardently to change the subject. But Tenika suddenly got much more interested.

"Tell me about those Black Irish," she said. She looked at Marta pointedly. "You're saying Marta is a Black Irish name?"

Kate wilted slightly. "I honestly don't know where my name came from," she admitted. "I think my mum just liked it. Anyway, Lizzy we haven't heard much about your story," she pressed.

"Oh, I haven't got that much to tell," Lizzy replied lazily. Her eyes were still closed in the sunlight. She yawned. "Anyway, I'm just grateful you're here, Marta."

Tenika stood up. "Better get back to it," she said tersely.

"Yep," agreed Lizzy, opening her eyes. "This just feels so good. I haven't actually been outside in days." She blinked at the realization. "Wow," she said softly. "I mean I ride my bike to work and stuff, but that's not like sitting in the sun."

"Do you ever get up to any of the parks or out to the beach?" Kate asked as Tenika headed back inside.

"Not really," Lizzy admitted. "At least not in the past year."

Kate looked at her curiously.

"My partner and I broke up last February," Lizzy continued. "It was pretty rough going, but I'm back." She smiled at Kate. "Anyway, yeah. I love the beach. I just haven't been there in a while."

Silence settled over the two women. Still neither moved a muscle, and no one spoke. Instead, they sat, savoring the moment.

"Why do you ask?" Lizzy finally asked. She looked at Kate, and Kate smiled at her.

"I'm looking for things we might do together," she explained. The warm realization that she'd just made a small play for Lizzy filled her mind. And it felt right.

Emboldened, Kate continued. "I like you," she said, gazing steadily at Lizzy.

Lizzy blushed and looked right back at her. "Good," Lizzy replied. Then she stood up and held out her hand to Kate.

"Come on," she said. "Let's go paint." Kate put her hand in Lizzy's and rose from the bench, feeling like she'd just been asked to dance. Then, just as casually, Lizzy released her hand as they walked inside.

Kate savored the brief linger of Lizzy's touch. For that one moment, it felt solid, warm and dependable—all things good and orderly in life. It also felt marvelously strong and somewhat electric.

Just as she knew it would.

*

The second coat was nearly done. Kate stood back, observing their work. The entire corner was now transformed. But something else had immediately became apparent; the rest of the garage looked like a dark, grimy mess.

"What do you think?" asked Lizzy, joining her.

"This corner looks amazing, but everything else…" Kate hesitated, holding her tongue, as she glanced around. After a moment, she added gently, "I'm sorry, Lizzy, but I think redoing the corner is probably not enough."

Lizzy folded her arms across her chest and furrowed her brow. "Hmm," she said. Then she called to her partner. "T? I think we need you here."

"One thing I've noticed," Kate continued, "other garages often have separate rooms for the customers."

"Some even have sushi bars," added Tenika, joining the conversation. "And freaking chair massages."

Kate blanched slightly. She was fairly sure they were on to her, but still she cautioned herself to stay focused. Flustering about

97

would do nothing for her now. "Do you see what I mean?" she asked Tenika. "Now this corner just makes the rest of the garage look a bit dreary."

"Mmm-hmm," she said. "That's what I've been saying all along. This place looks like hell."

"So," began Kate. "Shall we just paint the rest of it? It's only Saturday afternoon…" Her voice trailed off as the other two looked at her silently.

"Perhaps we could pull it off if the three of us worked tonight and tomorrow," Kate pressed on.

"And if we picked up a little, too. Fresh paint through the space would make a big difference."

"Oh, Marta, I don't know," Lizzy began dubiously. "We still have to get some furniture in the corner as well."

But suddenly, Tenika came to life. "I agree," she said. "For one thing, you bought enough paint to cover two more garages, Lizzy. So let's just keep going, right? You two do the prep and undercoat this afternoon on those other three walls, and I'll put stuff away and clean up the rest of it. Look," she said, pointing over her head. "Just paint the wall surface above the storage racks up to the ceiling. It will look way better."

Tenika continued. "I'll bring in some industrial cleaner and I can scrub the floor tomorrow while you guys add the second coat. Maybe I'll rent a power washer, too." She was now on a roll. "I'm sure we have more storage room in the back."

The three of them stood there, contemplating the overhaul. "You seriously think we can do all this?" Lizzy asked.

"We can do anything we damn well please," pointed out Tenika.

"And you said yourself that many hands make light work," noted Kate. "At any rate, it can't hurt."

"True enough," Lizzy said. "Okay. Let's see how far we get." Then she stopped for a moment. "You've already given us so much help, Marta. Are you sure you want to stay?" she asked. "I mean, you certainly don't have to."

"And miss all of this?" Kate asked with a laugh. "Of course I'm staying to help. Anyway, you need me."

"Oh, you know I do," Lizzy agreed quickly, and Tenika laughed out loud.

"Okay, you two, get to work," Tenika quipped.

Lizzy began pouring paint once again as she fought the blush that had come over her.

Kate, having completely forgotten about the dog in her charge, picked up a roller and once more began to work.

At this point, she could paint all night.

*

"Oh *sweet Jesus!*" Kate said as she glanced at her watch. She jumped up from their resting place with horror. It was just past seven p.m. and the kennel where she'd stashed Mr. Big was now closed for the night. "Damn it!" she declared, reaching for a nearby rag.

Kate called the number for the Canine Sanctuary, and listened to their voicemail message urging callers to try again in the morning. How could she have forgotten about Mr. Big?

"Is everything okay?" Lizzy asked, coming to her side. Tenika turned around from her spot washing brushes at the utility sink, and gave Kate an appraising glance.

"It's my boss's pug. He's been at a kennel all day," Kate muttered, as she hung up the phone. She glanced up at Lizzy. "I forgot to pick him up," she admitted.

Honestly, she'd been caught in a whirlwind for the past three hours, working and chatting alongside the two women. The mood was so uplifting, so relaxed and fun, there seemed to be all the time in the world. In fact, she hadn't felt this grounded or good in a long time.

"So, is that a bad thing? I mean someone's taking care of him, right?" Lizzy asked.

"Well, yes," Kate reasoned.

"It's like sleepaway camp, right? So he's with his dog pals," added Tenika. "He's probably happy as a clam," she added over her shoulder. Then she smiled at Kate.

For as much as Tenika nursed her suspicions, she'd grown a little fonder of her new acquaintance in the past few hours. It was starting to not matter exactly who 'Marta' was.

The three women had spent the last six hours painting a base coat across the rest of the garage, as well as the second coat on the conversation corner. It was obvious as they painted that they simply couldn't do the job without Kate.

Not only was she a competent, energetic worker with a good eye, she appeared to have an endless stream of ideas for them, all of which she freely shared. If she was with the competition, she was either working some master plan Tenika couldn't begin to figure out, or she really was just kind and generous.

A moment earlier, the three of them stood together admiring their work. "This color really looks good," Kate exclaimed. "It's warm and friendly."

"But not too blah," Tenika concurred. "I agree. It's amazing what a little paint will do."

"I kind of can't believe it," Lizzy said. "It's fantastic. So what do you have in mind for furniture, Marta?"

"Oh, a small couch, I suspect. You'll need a table and chairs. A rug, throw pillows, a little art. Perhaps some plants. And some nice lighting, as well. Something soft and friendly. A fringed lampshade sort of feel."

"But no Wi-Fi, no power strip," interjected Tenika. "Not if you want these ladies to break down and actually talk to each other. They're going to reach for their phones as it is."

"True enough," interjected Lizzy.

"But if we make the space warm and appealing enough, they might not. That's why I'm thinking a place for jigsaw puzzles. Or perhaps some tavern puzzles."

"Tavern puzzles?" Lizzy asked.

"They're interesting knots of tangled up steel rods about so big." Kate held up her hands to demonstrate the smallish puzzles. "And they're put together in such a way that you can unhook them from each other, if you have the patience."

"Another old Irish tradition?" Lizzy chuckled.

"Certainly not," said Kate, looking mildly offended. "They go back to the taverns of Colonial New England. And they give people something to do in an engaging way that isn't entirely preoccupying. So you could still nurse a pint and have a lovely chat at the same time. Or you might help a new friend figure one out. You could make a table card to that effect. Offer a prize for untangling one."

"I like that," Tenika volunteered. "Get people off their damn phones. We can give away an oil change."

"Exactly!" said Kate. "You get it."

"I like it, Lizzy," Tenika said. "I can see customers buddying up on this."

"Yep," Lizzy agreed. "I like it, too."

Once again, Tenika remarked to herself that this 'Marta' was alright. In fact, she was just a little bit of manna from heaven. Ogun was, indeed, doing his thing on their behalf. But then, Tenika had been faithfully lighting and relighting the candle in the half pineapple every day.

A moment later, she finished washing up and left the brushes to dry on the counter by the sink.

"I gotta get home. Delilah's been waiting on me for hours," she said to the others.

"Tell her 'thank you' for me. She has the patience of a saint," Lizzy said.

Lizzy and Kate watched her go, and as she passed by them, Tenika could feel the sexual tension building. Something was about to happen for sure, she mused. Maybe Ogun was working on a whole lot of fronts.

"Goodnight, ladies," she said gaily. "Don't do anything I wouldn't do."

"Tenika, what wouldn't you do?" asked Lizzy with a look of genuine stupefaction.

Tenika chuckled. "I'm just saying have a good night."

"Lovely night to you, Tenika. I enjoyed painting with you today," Kate added.

"As did I, my friend." Tenika paused and took Kate's hand; she looked her in the eyes. "Seriously. Thank you for all of this, Marta. You are a blessing to this place."

"Oh, it's a blessing to me," she replied. "Believe me."

*

The two of them watched Tenika head out. Then Lizzy turned to Kate. "Come to dinner with me tonight," she said. "I have a surprise for you."

Kate smiled at Lizzy. "A surprise?" she said. "I can't imagine what that would be."

"Well, you're not going to find out unless you say yes."

Kate looked up at Lizzy. Her green eyes were radiating kindness. "You don't have to get me any surprises," she gushed.

"No, I do. I have to thank you, Marta," Lizzy explained. "But it isn't that I have to. I mean, I want to! You've been amazing today. You're just amazing in general."

The two of them regarded each other silently. Kate wondered, yet again, if this was the moment to tell Lizzy the truth.

And once again, she rejected the notion. She needed just a bit longer.

"I accept," Kate said. "Happily."

"Good," Lizzy said pulling out her phone. She checked the time. "Let me go home and shower, then I'll pick you up. 8:30?"

"Okay," nodded Kate, allowing herself to be carried along by the rushing river of desire, longing, lust and love.

"Where do you live?" Lizzy asked, and suddenly Kate returned to Earth with a thud.

There was no way in hell she was giving her Mindy's address, not with the mailbox out front in the shape of a race car and the garish gold lettering above it that said 'Mindy Rose.'

"Meet me back here," Kate said quickly. "To save time." Lizzy appeared to accept this without question. Picking up her bag, Kate headed for the door. "See you in a bit," she said. "8:30."

"8:30," Lizzy repeated, not taking her eyes off Kate.

Kate was going to have to move it to get back on time. But given that her feet were not fully hitting the ground at this point, she didn't think it would be a problem. Kate smiled and took one last glance at Lizzy over her shoulder.

And the world smiled back at her through Lizzy.

Chapter Ten

"Wow," Lizzy said as Kate approached an hour and a half later. Kate felt a small flutter of excitement travel up from her belly.

Lizzy was now wearing her street clothing—clean jeans and a button down shirt in a beautiful shade of blue beneath a clean Carhartt jacket. Her nicely polished black oxfords and small turquoise stud earrings were lovely finishing touches. In fact, Lizzy looked downright sharp.

She was studying Kate appraisingly with her arms folded over her chest. Lizzy liked what she saw and smiled with appreciation. "Nice look," she said approvingly.

If you only knew, Kate thought with a smile. She'd raced home, torn apart her closet, agonized after trying a dress, then a skirt, then a shorter skirt, then back to a long skirt...because in Northern California the weather was totally transitional right now... She'd ended up in a summer dress with a warm cashmere button up sweater that showed just a bit of cleavage, pretty earrings and some nice heels.

Even so, the debate over what to wear continued in the car as Kate rushed back to Lizzy. Somehow the clothing she chose for this last-minute date seemed wildly significant.

Kate felt flustered and excited that Lizzy appreciated her effort.

"I thought you might like it," Kate answered boldly as she neared Lizzy. They stood silently, smiling at each other for just a moment. Then Lizzy offered her arm. "Let's walk back to my truck," she said. "I'll drive."

Kate took her arm, and together they walked along the side-walk contentedly. There didn't seem to be that much to say in that moment. Rather, there was a complicity. This was their evening to spend together exactly as they wished. Kate was eager to find out what would happen next.

When they both spoke, it was at the same time.

"I wanted—" began Lizzy.

"I'm curious—" Kate started.

They both laughed. "Go ahead," Kate offered.

"No, you go," Lizzy said.

"I wonder, where you're taking me?" Kate asked.

"I can't wait to show it to you," answered Lizzy. "But it's a surprise. I just hope you don't know it yet."

*

As it turned out, Kate was completely surprised. "I can't believe it," she said when they arrived at the restaurant. She turned and smiled broadly at Lizzy, her entire face lit with happiness. They were standing in front of the Irish pub at the bottom of Broadway.

"How on earth did you know about this place?" Kate asked.

"It's kind of new. I heard about it from a client last month," Lizzy explained.

"Can you pronounce the name?" asked Kate.

"I was going to get you to teach me how to say it. And explain it. What the heck does it mean, anyway?"

"*Sláinte.* Like Slon-cha. It's Irish Gaelic. It means 'good health,'" Kate explained. "You toast with it. Then everyone replies '*sláinte agad-sa.*'"

"Slon...cha?" Lizzy tested the word on her tongue.

"Not bad," Kate said approvingly with a light in her eye. "*Sláinte agad-sa.* But don't worry, Lizzy, there won't be a quiz 'til later."

Lizzy took her hand. "Come on," she said, leading Kate to the door. "Let's get our table."

The pub was predictably packed on a Saturday night. A slightly disheveled-looking set of musicians appeared to be taking a break as Kate and Lizzy found a table in the corner. A fire burned just across the room beneath a painting of T.S. Eliot, and a crowd three deep stood around the bar drinking Guinness on tap and talking. A brick wall with bookshelves added to the cozy spirit of the place, and it felt slightly damp in the room, as if the crowd had just stopped dancing.

"We got here just in time," Lizzy remarked, taking her seat on the small, rustic stool at the table.

The air was upbeat with laughter and the general pheremonal high of Saturday night near Jack London Square in Oakland.

"This is good, very good," Kate said, looking around. She wiped a tear from her eye with an embarrassed laugh. "Almost makes me a bit sad. It's that authentic."

Kate gave a satisfied sigh. "How could I not have known about this?" she wondered aloud. But then, of course, how could she? Kate had been firmly in the Mindy Rose micro-bubble for so long she'd forgotten about the rest of life.

Lizzy smiled at her. "Care for a Guiness?" she asked.

Kate glanced at the menu. "A Snake Bite!" she exclaimed. "Look at that. I haven't seen one of those since I left Dublin." She beamed up at Lizzy. "I really can't believe this place."

Nor could she believe Lizzy, who'd single-handedly just opened the door to what appeared to be an entirely new life. Glowing, Kate looked around the room, reveling in her newly improved luck.

When their drinks arrived, Kate felt that a toast was in order.

"*Sláinte,*" said Kate, raising her Snake Bite in Lizzy's direction.

"Yeah, slon-cha," parroted Lizzy. "Sorry I can't remember the other part."

Kate smiled. Sitting back, she realized she was utterly content. The last twenty-four hours had been the perfect snapshot of the life she'd come to California to find. Here she was, finally. She was out in the world with a truly kind, beautiful and trustworthy woman. Someone who actually cared enough to show her all of this.

As if on cue, the musicians picked up their instruments and once again began to play. They were seated around a small wooden table that held some empty glasses and a few pints of Guinness. One man played a fiddle and another kept time with a small, one-sided drum. A woman across the table played a guitar, while another woman played a wooden flute. The tunes they played were old Celtic, and the musicians eyed each other intently as they began to slowly get into the tune.

Suddenly, the music spun up and seized the room as the fiddle, the drum and the guitar kicked in. In no time, it became fast and furious, as if the musicians had suddenly come to life. Their tempo picked up even more as they modulated a key. Then the flute player threw in a racing, jubilant melody on top.

The crowd around the bar now began to clap in time as the music built. As if someone had just pushed the 'on' button, the chatting drinkers were transformed into a howling, clapping, unruly mob of dancers.

In no time, the entire pub joined them, leaping to their feet and clapping in time. Everyone became focused on the joy stream coming out of the stone-faced musicians, each of them equally intense as they followed one another's racing lead.

"I can't believe this!" yelled Kate to Lizzy with a laugh, and Lizzy just grabbed her hand.

Taking another pull of the glass of Irish whiskey she'd ordered, Lizzy stood up and pulled Kate to her feet. Together they joined the stomping, clapping whirl that pounded all around them.

People were now shouting, hopping, dancing and clapping, their arms raised in a sort of ecstatic frenzy as the band pitched up its music even faster.

As they swung into the final round, the flute player streaked across the top of the sound like a fast-moving bird, and the song carried on, minute after minute.

As she danced, Kate felt herself unfold, like a ragged piece of origami that had been folded and unfolded too many times. Now she was once again being smoothed out, all her wrinkles lost, all her corners perfect and sharp once more. She danced and spun with Lizzy, whose hand never left her own.

Kate looked at Lizzy dancing, and she suddenly realized she felt complete. It was as if she could die in the next minute, and the hard struggle of her life would now be instantly rectified. Here in this place, she was quite simply home.

She'd lost her tension, worries and her pain with good music and a little drink on a Saturday night, something she hadn't done since she'd left Dublin. Kate wondered idly where she had been all this time. Then, in the next breath, she wondered where Lizzy had been all this time, as well.

It all seemed so very right.

Finally the sweating, clapping, pounding maelstrom of the band, the song and the pub drew to a crashing conclusion. The crowd roared its approval as they made their way back to their tables. They looked up to see a waitress fighting her way through the crowd in their direction. They placed their dinner order and sat back in the thrall of a Saturday night moment.

Kate took Lizzy's hand, not wanting to let go. "Thank you," she said, shaking her head. "I had no idea any of this was here."

"How could you not have known?" Lizzy asked, entwining her fingers with Kate's.

"I've just…" Kate began, but then she stopped herself. Once again, she was reminded of what lay ahead that night—telling

Lizzy the horrible, but irrefutable truth. She shrugged off the thought. "I've been busy," she said.

"Being an accountant," observed Lizzy.

"That, or hiding from life," offered Kate. "Now I wish I'd paid more attention."

"But you're here now, and the night is young," Lizzy said, raising a glass. "And apparently, you're about to have Irish breakfast at nine o'clock at night. It sounds to me like you're getting exactly what you want."

"I haven't eaten boxty since I left Ireland, I can tell you that," Kate confirmed with a smile.

They touched their glasses as the music around them began in earnest once more.

It was time, for a while, to relax.

*

By the time they'd finished dinner, served to them by a jostled but determined waitress, they were complete. The two women had danced, drank and surrendered to the portent of Saturday night with everything they had.

Kate hadn't thought about Mindy, Mr. Big or even the persistent lie she was living for at least two hours. As a result, she felt fantastic.

Lacing her fingers once more through Lizzy's, she stepped out onto the sidewalk. "Now where?" she wondered aloud, shooting her date a look. Grabbing Lizzy's arm, she edged in a bit closer. She was turned on, refreshed and still caught up in the euphoria of the pub and its musical whirl.

"That was a downright saucy look you just gave me, Miss Marta," Lizzy said.

"Don't call me Marta!" Kate blurted.

"Oh?" Lizzy said, one eyebrow raised. "What should I call you, then?"

"Call me Kate," Kate announced. "That's my real name." But then she stopped herself as an electric jolt of pure fear ran down her spine. What the hell was she doing?

She couldn't tell Lizzy *now. No, no, NO!* She was too damn drunk for one thing. Even just one little Snake Bite was too much to deliver news this big.

When Kate finally told Lizzy the truth, she had to be completely serious and the time had to be entirely right. It was too important. "It's my Irish name," Kate now offered half-heartedly.

Lizzy looked confused. "So, what, people have two names in Ireland or something? Like your Catholic name and your street name?" she asked.

"Not exactly," Kate faltered. But at this moment, that was all she was going to say. "Let's not talk about it," she asserted. Pulling Lizzy closer to her side, she walked forward into the darker block up ahead of them.

"Hmmm," said Lizzy, following along. "We didn't actually think your name was Marta."

"No?" said Kate, still forging on straight ahead.

"It's not even remotely Irish."

"Right," Kate answered a little vaguely. Now she led Lizzy toward one of the dark, empty wholesale market bays on Franklin Street. The setting was rough and industrial, and suited Kate's own wild, reckless mood.

"Come here," she said, pulling Lizzy under the cover of the bay. Taking Lizzy's face in her hands, Kate kissed her hard. Lizzy responded by wrapping her arms around Kate and pulling her close as her tongue found its way inside Kate's mouth. They kissed. And they kissed.

"I can't sleep with you," Kate offered breathlessly as she abruptly pulled back. "I'm—" She stopped. And then, unexpectedly, she began to cry. "I'm sorry," Kate whispered, sinking back into her own confusion.

"What on earth?" Lizzy asked. "Hey, it's okay. I mean, you kissed me first, but who's counting?"

"No, no. I know," said Kate, looking up at Lizzy in the shadows of the bay. "I'm sorry. I can't get into anything at the moment. I wish I could. You are so...incredible," she concluded. "You're everything I've ever wanted," Kate admitted slowly.

Lizzy stroked her face as she looked at her. "I know. You're amazing, too. I feel it. We were meant to meet, Kate." They kissed again. This time Lizzy's hand on her back guided Kate to unfold a little more into her body. Kate could feel the heat rising and herself melting.

Somehow, she managed to pull back. "But I just can't..." Kate said apologetically.

"Kate," Lizzy repeated, looking down at her.

Kate looked up into Lizzy's eyes. "What?" she asked a bit dreamily.

"I was just trying on your name. *Kate.* Yeah, it feels much better than Marta. Definitely," Lizzy nodded her head. "You're definitely a Kate."

"You're not mad?" Kate asked, barely able to look at her now.

"Why would I be mad? You can't force a river, and you can't tell someone who to love. No matter how beautiful, interesting, fun or smart she is..." Lizzy's words became slower and slower as she began to finger Kate's long hair. Then, leaning over, she kissed Kate again. "Kate," she said softly.

"That's me," Kate replied, barely able to speak.

They kissed for another long moment, then simultaneously they both pulled back and looked at each other. They both seemed to have a lot to say. Kate cleared her throat. "Where are we parked?"

"Up Broadway," Lizzy said, still stroking Kate's hair. Then she shook her head, as if calming herself. "Okay, then," she said.

Stepping back, Lizzy offered Kate her arm. Once more they began to walk, this time in the direction of the truck. "You still want to help us tomorrow?" Lizzy asked. "I mean, it's totally cool if you don't. I would understand completely."

"Of course I do," Kate said. "If you don't mind."

"Mind? We'd both be thrilled if you showed up. And I promise I'll be perfectly behaved."

Kate smiled. "I'll tell Tenika my real name in the morning."

"She already knows your name isn't Marta."

"Really?" squeaked Kate as casually as she could. A new river of fear suddenly rushed through her body. She'd forgotten entirely about Tenika.

"T's pretty savvy, you know," Lizzy continued. "Anyway, she thinks you're working for the competition or something, but I told her that was ridiculous. Why would you be helping us so much if you were?"

"Oh, my," was all Kate could say. "That would be…" Her words trailed off as the lump of tension in her throat got significantly bigger. She could see Lizzy's truck just ahead, and she began advancing on it more and more rapidly.

"Anyway, we're going to kill it tomorrow," Lizzy carried on. "You want to help me pick out some furniture? I mean, for the corner we just painted," she added. "You could. If you want to."

Kate chuckled, in spite of herself. "Sure," she said, turning back to Lizzy. "I'd actually love to."

Still, Kate didn't know how she would get through the next twenty-four hours. Truthfully, her very worst suspicion had just been confirmed. There was no question about it.

She was definitely falling for Lizzy.

*

Lizzy lay on her back and stared at the darkened ceiling above her, unable to sleep.

Thoughts of feeling Kate in her arms, Kate's hair brushing her face, Kate's mouth on hers occupied her mind.

Lizzy hadn't been kept up by a woman in a very long time, and now here she was, held captive.

Frankly, it felt wonderful. Even if Kate had lied about her name.

Once more, Lizzy considered the subject of her desire. Unpredictable. Beautiful. Smart, Funny. Kind. Generous. And somehow unknowable. *Kate.* Even her name was exactly right.

She was just the sort of woman Lizzy went for every time, usually against her better judgment.

Lizzy knew exactly where this was going and she was secretly thrilled. As far as she was concerned, all of Kate's protests and fumbles and retreats were dust in the wind. If Kate wanted Lizzy to chase her, then she certainly would. Furthermore, she'd enjoy every minute of it.

Lizzy was certain. They would indeed be together, no matter what it took.

She rolled over and recalled, yet again, the moment their lips found each other in the dark. It was stunning, that kiss. Spectacular, really. It might have even been historically significant.

Really, it felt like the best kiss Lizzy had ever had.

And if kissing was that hot, connected, fervent—and every other positive adjective Lizzy could possibly think of—well, then, sex was undoubtedly going to be once in a lifetime.

Epic, even.

Lizzy had no idea what Kate's problem was at the moment, and frankly she didn't care. She knew enough about people to know that Kate was just as hooked as she was.

There was no turning back now. This was just the way of all things.

Chapter Eleven

K ate paced, the phone clamped tightly to her ear.

"No, I realize," she countered. "Something came up and I just couldn't get over—" She paused and listened. "An extra seventy-five dollars?" Kate croaked, swallowing hard.

The tinny voice on the other end carried on insistently.

Kate stopped dead. "One hundred and fifty dollars!" she exclaimed. "Just for today and yesterday?"

Only in the Bay Area, she thought grimly as she collected herself. "Fine," she continued smoothly. "I'll pay the fee when I pickup Mr. Big. Yes, I understand. By five o'clock."

Disconnecting, Kate put the phone down and rubbed her eyes. She needed every penny of what she'd hoped would be the last paycheck from Mindy. And now it would be one hundred and fifty dollars lighter.

Why did every last damn thing in her life have to fall apart at the same moment?

And why was she unable to sleep, unable to do nearly anything but surrender to thought after thought about Lizzy? Kate seriously had to get a grip.

The unthinkable had happened. She'd been drunk enough to tell Lizzy her real first name. And kiss her over and over. But Lizzy was never going to know the rest.

No, Lizzy was never going to find out who she actually was.

And if nothing else, this really was dizzying confirmation of exactly what Kate had been longing for. Of course, it could not continue. Not if she wanted to avoid living on the street.

After today and this one last encounter, there would simply be no more contact between Kate and anyone at Driven Garage. Today, she would finish what she'd started. She'd compensate for any pain she'd caused while working for Mindy by helping Driven stay open. Then she would walk away.

It was a matter of survival.

Then when she was ready, Kate would leave this godforsaken job. She would do it on her terms, with an apartment in her own name and a decent job waiting in the wings. Yes, she was going to do this whole thing like an adult. Then, and only then, would she actually tell Lizzy the truth about who she was and how she felt. If she had the courage.

In this moment, at least, Kate could feel her resolve coming back online.

Being alone had suited Kate just fine so far, she told herself. So why change things now?

*

Kate pushed the loaded roller of Mountain Mushroom latex up the wall of the garage and studied the cover that it gave. A blanket of thick, wet paint puckered under her stroke. So she rolled more, smoothing it out.

This was her practice now. Focus on painting and assiduously avoid Lizzy's rambling banter and easy laugh immediately to her left.

Still, as Kate worked, she couldn't help but glance at Lizzy painting just a few feet away from her. Each time she did, she was flooded with the most remarkable sense of calm. It was the calm she'd come to associate with these people and this place. And an undeniable sense of familiarity that Kate was now doing her best to ignore.

Lizzy seemed utterly unaffected by what had happened the night before. In fact, she was now humming a Tracy Chapman song under her breath and working along with her usual relaxed ease.

What Kate was most afraid of—besides telling them who she was—was that Lizzy would keep flirting with her. And so the tension would just keep building until, well…who knew what would happen?

But so far, Lizzy had been true to her word. She was, indeed, behaving perfectly. She was casual. Relaxed. Not one iota of sexual vibe in the air.

"Hey, y'all!" Tenika's voice cut through Kate's thoughts.

"Hello there," Kate replied as steadily as she could.

"Whatcha got, T?" Lizzy asked as she put down her roller. Tenika was lugging in a rented power washer and a gallon of industrial cleaner to wash the floor.

"We're going to make this place shine," she announced, putting the power washer down with a thud. "And I'm fricking thrilled!" But Kate wasn't listening. Instead, she was already strategizing about the best time to tell Tenika her real name.

She needn't have bothered.

"Yeah, so, T, turns out you were right all along," Lizzy continued. "Marta, here, isn't Marta. She's actually Kate." Lizzy smiled in her direction. "At least that's her Irish name. They get two names over there. Cool, right?"

T looked at Lizzy with raised eyebrows. "Seriously?" she asked. Then she shook her head. "Okay, Kate. Fine," she said dismissively. "What did I tell you?" Kate heard her add in a low voice to Lizzy.

Kate's throat contracted, and she felt a sudden well of tears. Now it occurred to her that coming back to Driven might have been a terrible idea. There was no way to avoid the fact that she had already caused harm. Tenika was right to be suspicious of her.

In this moment, she was a liar, and no better than Mindy Rose.

They painted in silence for a while. Kate could feel Tenika trying to size up the connection between her and Lizzy, wondering exactly what had happened last night.

Finally she spoke up as she hooked her washer to the sink tap. "So you two went out last night or what?"

Lizzy and Kate looked at each other. Glancing away, Lizzy smiled. "Yeah," she said. "Great time. We went to that Irish pub downtown. This place called *Sláinte*."

"You should have joined us!" Kate added in a jocular tone.

Tenika just looked at her and laughed. "Uh, I don't think so," she said.

"It's near Jack London," Kate continued, nonplussed.

"Super fun place," Lizzy continued. "Incredible music. Right across from Souley Vegan. You know it?"

"Can't say I do," Tenika said, as she attached the power washer hose to the work sink.

Again, there was silence. Finally, Kate spoke up. "I don't know why I didn't share my name with you," she said to Tenika as she shook her head remorsefully. "I'm sorry."

"I knew you were lying," Tenika said evenly. She looked up at Kate. "But no harm done, Kate. You're here now. That's what matters."

"Really. I am sorry," Kate repeated.

"Don't worry about it," Tenika said with a shrug. Then turning on with a roar, and she immediately set to her work spraying the garage floor clean.

Kate turned back to Lizzy, and for the first time all day, she allowed herself to look Lizzy in the eye, fully and completely. What she saw there disarmed her.

For all of her casual bluster, Lizzy's expression now was dead serious as she gazed back at Kate. There could be no mistaking what Kate saw. It was a look of complete and total surrender.

Lizzy was falling in love with her.

*

By the time they reached IKEA, Kate had a new philosophy. Rather than fight the palpable sexual tension that still hung between them, she would surf it instead.

Kate figured she really had no choice. She'd been given this day along with all the rest in her life so far. So why not look for the pockets of joy? Especially given that they would disappear in the near future.

As Lizzy drove, she closed her eyes and listened to the smooth cadence of the wheels as they hurried along 580. She noticed how Lizzy handled her truck with practiced ease and how comfortably she laughed and even sang as they drove.

Lizzy happily hummed along with Credence Clearwater Revival as she drove. It was Lizzy's effortless happiness and full-on embrace of joy that endeared her to Kate.

What was the worst that could happen? She either kept her resolve and never saw Lizzy again, or she told them both the truth and she never saw Lizzy again.

It was a lose-lose proposition Kate reasoned with herself.

With this new perspective, Kate relaxed and let go. In turn, everything became more of a psychedelic daydream. She noticed the slight bob of Lizzy's head as she drove and sang, the way her dark curls brushed her jacket as she made her way through the store ahead of Kate. And she noticed the way Lizzy navigated the endless maze of IKEA and its bright, shining surfaces in utter confusion.

"*What the...?* I could swear we were just here!" Lizzy protested as they stood at the intersection of rugs and bathroom furnishings. All around them, fellow nesters pushed carts or carried enormous blue bags stuffed with toilet brushes, cutting boards, pillows and light fixtures.

"I believe we go straight," Kate said, pointing ahead.

"Oh, you mean 'gayly forward?'" countered Lizzy, and they both laughed. Both of them were just old enough to remember the LGBTQ catchphrase.

Finally, they reached the sofas and armchairs section. Kate sighed as she stopped and surveyed the small sea of couches. The possibilities appeared endless, but nothing caught her eye.

Lizzy and I would never have these in our home. They're simply too cold. Where did that thought come from?

Kate folded her arms. "What do you think?" she asked, hoping to derail her current train of thought.

Lizzy put her hands on her hips and looked around. "Well, it's not to my taste," she said. "But if you like it…"

"I don't, actually," Kate replied. "They all look like something out of *A Clockwork Orange*."

"Exactly!" Lizzy agreed. "We want homey and nice, right?"

"Comfortable," Kate added.

Their eyes met and they smiled at each other. This time Kate could not turn away. She was held fast by Lizzy's gaze.

Impossible love had reared its head, yet again.

"But if you want to," Kate said slowly, her eyes still not leaving Lizzy's. "Pick out something. I mean, while we're here."

"Yeah," said Lizzy, gazing right back at her. "We should."

Still they just looked at each other. Lizzy swallowed, and finally Kate turned away.

"Anyway," she began vaguely.

Anyway what?

Lizzy, I have to tell you something, and I have to tell you right now, in the middle of IKEA's sofas and armchairs department. Before this can go one moment further, I have to tell you that I am the biggest, sketchiest liar in the world, and that my job is to take you down professionally. To destroy your business…

Kate exhaled, folded her arms crisply and returned to the business of finding a couch. "Do we want a love seat or a proper sofa?" she asked Lizzy over her shoulder, heading off among the couches.

Lizzy followed along dutifully. "I guess a love seat is what would fit," she said. "You measured?" she asked hopefully.

Kate nodded. "We need something no more than 73 inches wide. And a love seat is better for, well…"

"Conversation," Lizzy added earnestly.

"Exactly."

"Here," Kate said after a moment. They stopped in front of a small red couch with an unpronounceable Swedish name. It was the one cozy-looking love seat in the showroom, and its slashed price tag indicated it had been part of the previous year's line. "This one will do."

"Yeah," Lizzy agreed. She nudged the couch with the toe of her boot. "I guess it's homey enough. Shall we give it a try?"

"Okay," Kate agreed hesitantly. The two of them sat down awkwardly on the love seat. Their knees touched for one brief moment and then separated immediately. Gingerly, Kate rose again to her feet.

"Very nice," she mumbled.

"Yeah. It's, uh, fine," said Lizzy. "Comfortable! Let's get it."

"Sure," said Kate. "Do you want to see the price?"

Lizzy shook her head. "Whatever it is, we can't afford it. But we're at IKEA, so how bad can it be?"

"Okay," Kate said, "let me get the details." Then she took a photograph of the love seat's label with her phone.

Lizzy smiled at her. "Good thinking," she said. Then putting her hands in her pockets, she rocked back and forth for a moment. Finally, she shook her head and looked at Kate "This is impossible," she sighed. "I mean, I'm trying here, Kate. But you're just so damn beautiful."

Kate closed her eyes, as if to squeeze out Lizzy's words. She couldn't stand to listen to them.

"Please, Kate …" Lizzy said. Her voice trailed off to silence.

"We'd better get down to the register," Kate said evenly.

"Yeah, okay," said Lizzy stiffly. "Sorry."

Quietly, they walked on in search of the cashier. And the exit.

*

The ride back to the garage was mostly silent. In the back, the enormous box holding the pieces of the couch bumped along behind them.

"Good thing you have a truck," Kate blurted, hoping to ease the tension.

"Yep," Lizzy agreed. "Made for trips like this."

They drove on.

Finally, as they neared the knot of traffic at the Maze, Lizzy turned to her. "Kate," she said.

"What?"

"I don't mean to pester you," Lizzy looked over at her, "but I need to know if I did something to offend you."

Kate closed her eyes. There it was. A simple request for honesty.

"No," she said, her eyes fastened on the passing scenery. "You didn't do anything, Lizzy. It's all on me. I have a complicated situation."

"It's someone else then?" Lizzy asked.

Kate sighed. "In a manner of speaking, but not how you think." She looked at Lizzy with true sympathy. "I'm sorry. I just can't get into this with you."

Silence ticked on as the traffic edged forward.

"You have been more than kind to me, Lizzy. I really do think you're wonderful," Kate reassured her.

"But not wonderful enough," Lizzy said staring at the windshield. Kate glanced over and noticed a tear sliding down Lizzy's cheek.

"Lizzy, please," she said, reaching for her hand. "This isn't about you."

But Lizzy would not take her hand. Instead, she stabbed at the errant tear with the back of her hand and gave an embarrassed laugh. "It's fine!" she protested. Clearing her throat, Lizzy picked up speed. "It's fine," she repeated with a shrug. "No biggie. Let's just forget any of this happened."

"Okay," agreed Kate.

They drove on, utterly silent in the fractured peace of a Sunday afternoon.

*

"I think we just have to screw the legs on," Lizzy asserted. "Did you see them?"

"I'm sure they're around here somewhere," Kate replied, peering into the enormous box the couch came packed in. "Wait, they're in the bottom."

It was a relief to have something to focus on. And as IKEA assembly instructions went, this one was on the easier side. Still, it had taken Lizzy the better part of half an hour to get the screws in at the right angle to make the couch's components fit correctly.

Immersing half of her body in the huge cardboard box, Kate finally extracted the small bag of plastic legs from the bottom. "Here!" she said, handing them to Lizzy.

Their mode had now shifted to jovial workmanship. Lizzy joked. Kate smiled. They worked on, uninterrupted in the quiet of the garage. Tenika was gone for the day, her work complete, and the clean floors were rapidly drying.

Driven garage was, indeed, transforming before their eyes.

The two women screwed the plastic legs in place, then gingerly flipped the couch frame over. Kate unwrapped the last of the couch cushions and tucked them into place as Lizzy pulled the assorted throw pillows they'd purchased from a pair of plastic bags.

Sitting there in front of the still drying Mountain Mushroom walls, the couch looked bright, crisp and inviting. Underneath it, a bright green rug with yellow and red daisies looked equally fresh, as well.

"Damn," Lizzy said. She glanced around at the newly painted walls throughout the garage, and the neatly organized shelves they'd worked on together. "This is fantastic. I mean, I barely recognize the place. Thank you so much…again!" she gushed.

"I wanted to help," Kate replied. And it was true. She did.

Lizzy continued to gaze around the garage. "All of this makes the place look bigger, don't you think?"

"It does," Kate agreed.

Lizzy's eyes came to rest on the couch. "Shall we?" she asked, glancing at Kate.

"Oh, all right," Kate said, primly. She took a seat on one side of the couch and crossed her legs. Lizzy landed easily beside her and sprawled out, giving the couch a comfort test. She closed her eyes.

"Very nice," she said with satisfaction.

"It is," agreed Kate. She glanced over at Lizzy. "It was a fun day," she said, feeling a little melancholy.

"Yeah," Lizzy said, looking at her. "I knew it would be."

Kate swallowed, once again fighting back the mixture of tears and serious lust that was piling up inside of her.

Why? Why the hell did any of this have to happen?

Screw it, Kate suddenly thought with abandon as the last of her resolve drained away. She'd done nothing but be a 'good girl' for as long as she could remember. As she sat on the couch beside this supremely good and attractive woman, the chief of so-called enemy territory, she decided she was done with that.

Their knees touched and this time Kate did not move her leg. Instead, she reached for Lizzy's hand. Lizzy in turn reached for her. And then they were in each other's arms.

Kate felt her lips touch Lizzy's as she closed her eyes and opened herself to the experience. Kate's hand found its way up into the great dark thicket of Lizzy's hair and pulled her closer. Lizzy followed willingly.

Lizzy sighed happily as she kissed Kate more and more deeply, and Kate ran her hands through Lizzy's curls. Lizzy reached for Kate's breast, and Kate responded with a small moan of pleasure. The mountain of desire that had been building since the day they'd met now crested and peaked. Kate realized she could soon be making love with Lizzy on the brand new couch in Driven Garage.

"Oh…" Kate stammered, pulling back. But the words 'I can't' got stuck somewhere in her throat and refused to emerge.

Lizzy stroked her face. "What?" she whispered. Taking Kate's face in her hands, Lizzy tenderly kissed her hair and her forehead and her cheeks and her nose again and again.

"It's so…" Kate said without finishing her sentence.

"I know," said Lizzy, leaning in to kiss her once more. "I knew it would be."

Kate closed her eyes and surrendered to the sheer power of Lizzy's embrace, her mouth and her hands. Nothing else in the world seemed to even exist in that moment. Kate realized she could stay there for hours.

There was simply no stopping it.

*

"What time is it?" Kate asked groggily. She sat up and looked around.

Lizzy regarded her with sleepy amusement, and she yawned and stretched. The two of them had fallen asleep on the new couch. Kate's head had been in Lizzy's lap, and now she remembered the slow slide down to the bliss of her lap, and how right it felt to be attached to Lizzy's body. How incredibly comfortable and comforting that lap was.

Lizzy reached over and smoothed Kate's hair with the hand that had been draped over her hip. "You're all rumpled," she said.

Kate blinked and yawned as she sat up. At least their clothing was still on, that was good.

How could I have fallen asleep?

But, she had. The simple serenity of being in Lizzy's embrace unlocked her, opened her up and set her straight.

Kate pulled her sweater to herself a little more tightly. "Okay," she said, apropos of nothing.

The moment of Lizzy's hands running over her body shot through her memory, releasing a rush of endorphins. Considerable heat spread through her groin once again.

Lizzy straightened her shirt. "Do I look okay?" she asked.

"You look like a highly seductive garage owner with a gorgeous smile," Kate replied.

"Okay, I'll take that," said Lizzy with a laugh. Standing up, she pulled Kate to her feet. "Lest we go places we don't want to go," Lizzy explained. Then she hesitated. "I mean, I certainly do. But you said...you know..."

"That I can't date you. And I'm afraid that I still can't," Kate added gently, looking at Lizzy with genuine sadness. "But I'm going to work on that. And I'll get back to you. Is that okay?"

Lizzy leaned in for a small, soft kiss. "Good enough for me." she said.

Reaching for her phone, Kate now glanced at it. "Six o'clock!" she cried with alarm. "It's six! Shit!"

"What's at six o'clock?"

"The dog! I forgot to pick up the blasted dog—*again!*" she howled. Kate now began grabbing her things and stuffing them into the canvas bag she'd brought with her. "I was supposed to get Mr. Big at five. I have to get out of here!"

"The dog's name is Mr. Big?"

"It's a pug, my boss's Pug. I...oh sweet Jesus! *I am so screwed!*

I am *beyond* screwed," Kate rambled grimly as she jammed her feet back into her sneakers. She looked around wildly, panic rising in her voice. "Where's my purse?"

Lizzy held it out. "Easy, Kate, please. Breathe," she said. "I'll walk you out. Is Mr. Big seriously a dog's name?"

"Yes!" Kate said, trying to manage her panic. She stopped and took a breath. "She's coming back tomorrow morning first thing and I have to have the dog there. She can't know I parked him at the kennel all weekend, and she definitely can't know I was—"

"Wait. Who's coming back tomorrow?" Lizzy asked.

"My boss. I live with her. It's strictly platonic, but she's hell to deal with. She's—" Kate stopped herself, realizing she'd probably already said too much.

"Anyway, who knows when the kennel opens up in the morning?" she continued as she rushed for the door of the garage, one shoe still in hand.

"Why are you racing out of here?" Lizzy asked reasonably. "Sounds like you've already missed picking up the dog."

Kate stopped as she reached the door, then she turned around to face Lizzy. She sighed. Leaning over, Kate put her foot in her remaining sneaker and tied it.

"I'm sorry," she said, as she stood upright. Then she walked to Lizzy and put her hands on Lizzy's waist. She looked up into her eyes. "Every last minute this weekend has been amazing. I'm so grateful I got to know you," she said.

Lizzy nodded. "Me, too," she said quietly. "But, hell, I should be thanking you because *you're* amazing, Kate. You're an incredible woman."

"So are you," replied Kate with sorrow.

They looked at each other for another long moment. Then stepping up on tiptoes, she allowed herself a final, deep, drawn out kiss with Lizzy—the sort of kiss a person might remember.

"Bye," she said, only inches from Lizzy's mouth.

"Wait, am I going to see you again?" Lizzy asked.

"I hope so," Kate replied. Then she smiled, as if to assuage her vagueness.

"I'll text." Lizzy said.

"Okay," Kate said. Then she turned and left in a whirl of angst.

Lizzy shook her head as she watched her go. Giving a long sigh, she pulled out her key ring.

Pausing at the door of the garage for a moment, Lizzy looked around at the clean, orderly and freshly painted space. It looked infinitely better.

It looked like a place that might actually succeed.

Chapter Twelve

"That will be $225," said the woman on the other side of the counter. She eyed Kate malevolently.

Dutifully, Kate handed over the required cash. If there was one thing Kate hated right now, it was her life. And most especially, she hated her job.

A moment later, Mr. Big appeared, snuffling along and completely oblivious to the pain his very existence had caused. Kate glanced at her watch. She had exactly seven minutes to get back to the house before Mindy was due to arrive.

"Let's go, Mister," Kate said, pulling him through the door. She picked up her pace on the sidewalk, breaking toward the car in a half-run. But at that moment, Mr. Big suddenly had to sniff. Planting his little pug feet, he resisted Kate's tugs on the leash. "Come on, Mr. Big. Come on…" she cajoled.

Mr. Big looked at her, unimpressed, and went back to sniffing his preferred patch of grass.

"Mr. Big, come on!" Kate wailed. Then looking both ways, she did the unthinkable and grabbed the small dog by the scruff of his neck. Holding him like a football, she now ran toward her car as the dog squirmed and groaned out a series of muffled yips and barks. She reached the vehicle just as he broke free and landed on the sidewalk with a plop.

Kate opened the door and Mr. Big growled at her. "Get in,

you little piece of shite," she hissed at the dog. Giving her one last dirty look, the dog climbed in and folded himself on the floor of the back seat. Pulling at her seat belt as she backed up, Kate took off, her tires practically screeching.

She had three minutes left to get home.

*

"This is *crazy!*" Tenika exclaimed as she peered out the door of the garage. She was looking at the line of women snaking their way down the street. More than a dozen had already gathered and it wasn't even eight o'clock. "Lizzy, how much coffee have we got?"

"Forget coffee, I hope we have enough engine oil," Lizzy said as she hurriedly yanked bottles out of the back storage area. "We're low on synthetics! T, how'd we get low on synthetics?"

"Well, I'm opening the door, sister. I say it's time to let the business back in here," Tenika announced as she raised the garage door with a flourish. "Hey, y'all! Come on in!" she called. "Coffee's on and it's a new day!"

And one by one, they came. Young tattoo-covered dykes stood studying their phones in line alongside older, heavyset women who'd known each other forever. They chatted among themselves convivially.

All of them came with the same goal—get their lube job discount and enter the romantic night out raffle.

And they stayed.

Within a matter of moments, six women were ensconced in the conversation corner while another three sat out on some folding chairs on the sidewalk. A playlist called 'Upbeat Morning' poured out from the Bluetooth speaker Kate had insisted they buy, and the garage hummed along at optimum speed. Lizzy and Tenika moved easily from car to car, with Tenika running to the cash register periodically to ring people up.

Every once in a while, Lizzy glanced over at the conversation corner. Everything she saw was positive. Two women were looking particularly cozy on the new red couch while another two worked on a jigsaw puzzle together at the table. Their customers were, indeed, connecting. Which was exactly what Kate had predicted would happen.

Lizzy shook her head and smiled. Kate's fairy dust was working.

*

"*Shit!*" Kate muttered under her breath. Pulling up to her parking spot on the street below the house, she saw Mindy standing in the driveway with her arms crossed and a sour look on her face.

Evidently, she'd been waiting for them.

"Welcome home!" Kate called, trying to muster up a cheerful tone. Mr. Big scrambled out of her car and ran for his owner's arms as the gate swung open.

Mindy Rose bent down to scoop him up. "Mommy's home, my little Mister!" she squealed as the dog licked her face appreciatively. Then, standing up, she leveled a look in Kate's direction.

"Where the hell were you?" she demanded.

"Oh, we just went out for a bit," Kate said. "Sorry to miss your arrival."

Mindy cocked her head. "No, really, Kate. Where were you?" she repeated. Her tone implied she needed a full accounting of all missteps, with appropriate punishment to come.

Kate sighed. There really would be no getting out of this. "Ah, well, you see, Mindy," she began. "I had to pick Mr. Big up. He was at the kennel last—"

"A kennel? Mr. Big was at some *kennel?* Are you kidding me?" Mindy hissed. "What is the point of having you here if you can't even follow simple instructions? I specifically said no kennel, Kate. Never, ever! Haven't you ever heard of kennel cough? Those are very dangerous places!"

Mindy held the dog up and inspected him closely. "Are you okay, my little man?" she murmured, kissing his head. Then she wrapped her arms around him protectively.

"Mr. Big should never be stuck in some terrible kennel. Christ!" she continued in disgust. Then turning away, Mindy began to trudge up the hill to the house with the dog still in her arms.

Now Kate stopped, uncertain of how to proceed. Should she just quit right now, like every fiber in her being was screaming for her to do? Or should she continue to take the measured approach? The safe approach. The approach she'd been trying to talk herself into.

In that instant, Kate hoped that Mindy would just fire her. Which would, of course, be a massive relief, albeit inherently dangerous. There would be no forthcoming unemployment checks from the U.S. Government and certainly no severance pay.

No, Mindy probably wouldn't fire her. They'd been together too many years and Mindy needed her.

Kate knew everything about her boss—from the type of underwear she preferred to the silent, crushing defeat Mindy had suffered after that last trip to the hospital. She'd seen the brain scans, and they weren't pretty.

It was something they didn't discuss, and the media didn't know about. It was an unspoken rule. No one could ever know about Mindy's CTE or her brain degeneration. But that's how it was with a disease that had no cure, no drugs and no therapy. You tried to pretend it wasn't there.

Kate felt massively sorry for Mindy. She'd seen her go from the unstoppable world-class race car driver to a beaten, empty person who still craved the limelight. So Mindy's now frequent rages were rendered all the more disturbing to Kate. They'd become far more serious and frequent since her last high-speed crash. And they were irrefutable evidence of her brain damage.

Kate stood in the driveway, unable to move and unable to decide where to go or what to do next. At that moment, her mind felt thoroughly jammed. She was screwed, no matter which direction she turned. There was no way to win this game, nor was there any way to save face with Mindy Rose. Or even to kindly, compassionately quit.

How would Mindy get along without her? There were many who would take this job. But who would keep it once they knew the truth about their erratic, dangerous boss?

No one.

Still, the fact remained that Kate had finally gone one step too far, and now she was out of options. And Mindy Rose didn't even know the full extent of her crimes. Hearing a soft ping, Kate pulled her phone from her bag. Lizzy had just texted a photograph.

A half-dozen women sat easily chatting and smiling around the table and on the couch in Driven's conversation corner. There was a plate of half-eaten cinnamon rolls in front of them, and assorted coffee cups were scattered around. They appeared to be having a lovely time.

"It's working," Lizzy wrote. "All because of you."

Stashing her phone in her purse, Kate closed her eyes against the cognitive dissonance that now filled her head. Horrifyingly, tears began to slide down her face. She couldn't cry now. Not if she was about to go talk to Mindy.

Kate needed to pull herself together. Sniffing hard, she wiped her face with the sleeve of her sweater and prepared for the worst.

Then slowly, she began to climb the hill to whatever fate lay ahead.

*

Kate opened the kitchen door as quietly as she could. She half-expected Mindy to be standing there, hands still furiously parked on her hips.

Yet, there was no sign of Mindy, which was also typical. Kate suspected that at this point Mindy simply enjoyed the game of terrorizing Kate. It appeared she'd become nothing more than a chew toy for Mindy, just like Mr. Big's tattered, but beloved Snuffy Bear.

Putting her hand on the refrigerator door, Kate stopped herself.

Why not just do it? she chided herself. *Just walk up to Mindy Rose, wherever she is in this godforsaken house, and just flat out quit. You owe that woman nothing…*

But, of course, this wasn't entirely true. Kate owed Mindy her last seven years of U.S. residency and employment. That certainly counted for something.

Still, the voice of encouragement continued. *She'd be fine. She was always fine. And you'll be fine. When you look at the entirety of your life, when have you not been fine?*

Kate tried to reason with herself. If she did actually quit, then she could run, not walk, right back to the waiting arms of Lizzy, who'd all but guaranteed the promise of more love, more fun and more life.

Hadn't she?

Kate stood stock still in the middle of the kitchen, reconstructing Lizzy's exact parting words.

She could see her clearly now, standing up from their beautiful, cozy nest of intimacy on the new IKEA couch. *"Lest we go places we don't want to go,"* Lizzy had said. Then she added. *"I mean, I certainly do."*

Kate inhaled sharply. Did this mean Lizzy actually wanted a relationship? Or was it just sex? Was Kate just barking up a tree that wasn't necessarily real?

Lizzy had never told her she wanted to date her in so many words. And Kate certainly wasn't going to go asking. That would require telling truths that, at this point at least, were still too painful and frightening to tell.

The more Kate thought about, the more she realized a grim fact. Lizzy was actually fairly non-committal so far. Yes, she was attracted to Kate, but was she actually serious about it? If Kate actually made the break and quit her job, it was entirely possible that Lizzy could just up and disappear.

Then where would she be?

Pulling the orange juice out of the refrigerator, Kate closed the door. Then she shook off her thoughts, pulled out her phone and deleted Lizzy's text and the attendant photograph.

There would be no quitting today.

Chapter Thirteen

"What just *happened* here?" Tenika declared with a happy laugh. "That was completely off the hook!"

"You got that right," Lizzy concurred. "Beer?" She was making a beeline for the fridge now that the last customer was finally gone and the door was bolted. The first day of their new campaign had been a wild, unprecedented success.

"Yes, ma'am," replied Tenika, now taking a seat at the cash register. She opened up a screen on the day's receipts. "How long's this promo going?" she asked, peering at the numbers.

Lizzy popped the top on two amber ales. "Six more days. How do we look?"

A wide smile broke out on Tenika's face. "We just did 23 oil changes, girlfriend. Six more days of this and we are rock solid. And we just booked out the whole week after the promo in repairs. Damn, that's good!"

"Hella good!" Lizzy agreed. She handed Tenika a cold beer and two looked at each other and grinned. "So you think we're gonna be okay, then?" she asked.

"We're gonna be just fine," Tenika confirmed. Then she raised her beer. "To Ogun, who is totally workin' it right now."

"To Ogun," Lizzy agreed, clicking bottles with her partner. "And to Kate."

"To Kate," Tenika echoed with a shake of her head. "I think I may be more into that woman than you are right now."

Lizzy chuckled, and they each took a long, cold pull from their beers.

"Yeah, she's pretty amazing," Lizzy said, blushing slightly. "I mean, well, you know…"

"You're gone," Tenika observed.

"Yep."

Tenika shook her head and smiled. "To love," she said, touching her bottle to Lizzy's once more. "For better or for worse."

"That poor woman," Lizzy continued. "She forgot to pick up Mr. Big because she was helping us, and now she's got hell to pay. It's her boss's dog, and—"

"Wait, wait, wait," interrupted Tenika, sitting up in her chair. "Mr. Big? That's seriously the dog's name?"

"Yeah. He's a little pug, I guess."

"Oh, noooo…" Tenika wailed, putting her bottle down. She looked at Lizzy intently. "No, no, no. Her boss has a pug named Mr. Big. You're not kidding me about this?"

"No! Why would I kid?"

"Lizzy," Tenika leaned and spoke very slowly. "Mindy Rose's fucking dog is Mr. Big."

"Mindy Rose? *The* Mindy Rose?"

"Our goddamn competition!" Tenika spat. "The very same fucking Mindy Rose who's actively trying to run us out of the business right now! Jesus, Lizzy, I told you this woman couldn't be trusted."

"Come on, T!" Lizzy protested. "How do you know this? There are probably lots of little dogs out there named Mr. Big."

But Tenika didn't respond. Instead, she was now on the garage's computer, madly searching Google.

"Here," she said after only a moment. Lizzy peered over her shoulder. There before them was the sunglasses-clad face of Mindy Rose. She was coming out of a store with her pug on a rhinestone-studded leash. "Race car driver Mindy Rose with her beloved pug, Mr. Big," read the caption.

Lizzy looked at the image wordlessly.

Tenika sat back and folded her arms. "Proof," she said after taking another pull from her beer. "We know she lives in Oakland. And we know she's got a garage. And I can pretty much guarantee there aren't a ton of pugs in the East Bay named Mr. Big."

"Wow," Lizzy finally said, the wind partly taken out of her. "I don't know, T. I think it's probably okay. If this is really her boss, Kate hates working for her. So maybe that's why she helped us."

"Sure. Or maybe she was scoping us out. Doing a little recon for the enemy," Tenika proposed. "It looks like she's playing you, Lizzy. Maybe she sweetened you up just to get access. I mean, you have to admit, she got a damn good look at our operation."

"Yeah, but what about today?" Lizzy countered. "If it wasn't for Kate, none of that would have happened. She has totally helped us *stay* in business. Anyway, I know for a fact she detests her boss."

"So why doesn't she quit?" Tenika asked.

Lizzy couldn't answer. "I don't know," she admitted with a sigh. "I honestly have no idea."

Tenika shook her head. "We've got a problem," she said. "No matter how rosy this all looks right now. No matter how Kate feels about her job, she still works for Mindy. And she knows way too much about us."

Lizzy sighed. Then she drained the rest of her beer. "I'll call her," she said, ignoring the fact that Kate had not responded to any of her texts today.

"Okay," Tenika said. Then she shook her head one more time. "I knew something was up with that chick," she said.

"Yeah, but seriously. Kate's a good person. I know she is," Lizzy continued.

Tenika leveled a look at Lizzy. "Baby girl, I don't underestimate the power of lust to totally screw up your wiring. And I do mean yours in particular."

Lizzy was quiet now. Her friend was right. She'd definitely been to the Department of Faulty Wiring before.

Lizzy sighed and shook her head. "Okay," she resolved.

She was, for the moment, undone.

*

"Mr. Big, come *on*," Kate hissed, pulling on the obstinate dog's leash. At this moment, she was walking the dog along Skyline Drive in the dark.

It had been a hard day. Mindy was spooked by the lines of customers waiting outside Driven Garage. Not surprisingly, she'd cruised by Driven, surveying the success of their promotion. It was typical of Mindy to get squirrelly and obsessive at times like this.

Consequently, Kate had been forced to deny there was success over at the competition. She'd even offered to go back, herself, in the afternoon to check the status of the lines. It was only because Mindy had wall-to-wall meetings for the rest of the day that she agreed to let Kate go in her stead.

So Kate set off, a host of butterflies swirling in her gut. At first, she used the time to go anywhere but Driven. She lunched at Whole Foods. And she drove around uptown for a while, observing the techies and the hipsters out in the sunshine on their lunch breaks. Finally, she could avoid it no longer.

Kate got off at the Powell Street exit of 580, her heart beating wildly. As she cruised casually up San Pablo, the Driven sign came into view. In that moment, Kate was reminded of how she'd come here with her flat tire on that first fateful day.

At that point, Driven just seemed like another innocent business that had strayed into Mindy's crosshairs. But now, Kate knew the truth. Driven was far more than just a garage. It was also her personal path back to redemption, but only if she was willing to choose Box A instead of Box B.

Then reality was plain as day, right in front of her. It was two o'clock in the afternoon and seven women stood in line outside of Driven, waiting patiently for their Valentine's Day lube jobs. Her plan had succeeded. Driven was, most likely, going to be just fine.

Kate drove on, her heart still pounding. Lizzy, potentially one of the most significant relationships in her life, the very one she'd come to believe she'd been waiting for all this time, was in that garage at that exact moment, pouring motor oil into a customer's car. Lizzy had no idea she was even here. Nor did Lizzy have any idea who she actually was.

Kate imagined Lizzy in her grease-covered overalls, her beautiful, dark head bent over an open engine. Lizzy, whose warm brown eyes poured nothing but affection into Kate's empty cup.

Lizzy, who blushed whenever she saw her.

"Hey!" she imagined Lizzy would say with delight, if Kate had the courage to walk in. It was that warm, inviting 'hey' that Kate longed for more than anything right now, spoken with Lizzy's tantalizing, slightly husky voice.

But, no, Kate would keep driving, because she had to. Though she'd be damned if she was going to snap a photo of the crowd outside of Driven like Mindy wanted. That was entirely too much.

Let Mindy think that the sale was just a flash in the pan, a so-so success. Let Mindy strangle on a few lies for a while.

That suited Kate just fine.

The dog turned and looked at her, now in the dark, and began leading her back toward the house. Kate followed.

She'd done what she could for one day. She'd dutifully deleted every one of Lizzy's texts as they'd come in, without answering a single one. At first, they had a celebratory tone, as Lizzy sent pictures of their success. By the end of the day, however, she sent a text that sounded worried.

"Everything okay on your end?" was all it said.

Then Kate heard nothing more from Lizzy. And that was the hardest thing of all. Yet again, she had successfully pushed away the possibility of love. She had to, out of nothing more than fealty to Mindy. After all, she was still her employer.

The gates to Mindy's house swung open, and the dog trotted happily up the driveway.

What in God's name am I doing?

Honestly, Kate had no idea.

*

Mindy stood at the kitchen sink, and looked out over her lawn. This was her life, she thought bleakly.

Nice house. Nice yard. Pretty garden. Decent grass. She was even driving a BMW I8 Roadster with custom paint. Technically, she had everything she'd ever wanted.

So why was she so damned nervous all the time?

It had everything to do with Kate, of course. Kate was changing before her eyes. She could feel it. Like just now, when she'd offered to take the dog for a walk. There was none of the usual nattering small talk and fluffy pleasantries. Kate couldn't even look Mindy in the eye. Instead, she just silently leashed him up and left.

That was strange. Very strange. It was as if Kate was angry about something. But what on earth did she have to be angry about? They were doing quite well with the new garage and their new life. Stunningly well, if Kate had even bothered to notice.

No, Kate had lost her gratitude, Mindy decided. She'd forgotten everything Mindy had done for her—the nice house in the hills, the health insurance, the job security all these years. Clearly, Kate had forgotten all of it. Instead, she'd turned into just another entitled Californian.

Because that was the thing—Kate seemed oddly checked out. Like she really couldn't care less how they did. Mindy walked to the living room window now, and watched Kate and Mr. Big walk up the driveway. Kate's countenance was glum. In fact, she looked miserable.

It was time to find out exactly what was going on.

"So?" Mindy asked as Kate pushed the kitchen door open. The dog scampered in before her.

"So what?" she asked.

"You didn't get back to me about the crowd at Driven today. There was one, I assume."

"Oh!" Kate flustered a bit. "Not really. I'd hardly call it a *crowd*, per se."

"But you took a photo."

Kate looked up sharply. "Oh, well, actually…" She hesitated. Then she looked up at Mindy. "I didn't."

"I told you to take a photo," Mindy reminded her.

Now Kate's tone grew frosty. "And I said I didn't."

"What the hell is wrong with you?" Mindy blurted, her voice rising. "You're not even doing your job anymore!"

"I am doing my job, Mindy," Kate continued evenly. "Just not all of it."

"And that does me no good. No good—do you hear me?" Mindy's voice rose up as she took a menacing step towards Kate. "You work for me, Kate—it's not the other way around. Dammit!" Mindy yowled in anguish. "I ought to just fire you right now."

"Fine," said Kate calmly. "Go ahead."

Mindy stopped and blinked. *Fine?*

Kate had just told her to fire her.

Wobbling slightly, Mindy took a step back on her kitten heels and looked Kate up and down. Then shaking her head, she pulled herself up and stalked out of the kitchen, saying nothing more.

Clearly, she was losing Kate.

And if there was one thing Mindy hated, it was losing.

*

Lizzy turned off the sink and placed the dripping plate in her drainboard. Dinner had been spaghetti and meatballs for one, with a side of National Public Radio.

All night long, she'd been bothered by Kate's lack of response. But she knew the rules of the game by now, after all these years of the lesbian approach-and-retreat. Or just the approach-and-stay.

Really, she'd been hoping this relationship would quickly fall into the second category because Kate was, well, a keeper. She was clearly a cut above the usual sort of women who made trouble in Lizzy's life. Even if she *did* work for the competition.

No, Lizzy still maintained that Kate had a pure and shining heart. She could feel it. Which made Tenika's belief that Kate was a spy for Mindy Rose all the more troubling. How could she have lied to her about something like this?

It made no sense. Unless, of course, Kate really was trying to break free from her job. That would at least explain her unavailability. Again and again, Lizzy replayed their conversation in the truck.

"It's someone else then?" Lizzy had asked.

"In a manner of speaking, but not how you think." Kate had said.

Now Lizzy sighed and snapped the dishtowel back into its spot on the rack. Of course, Kate couldn't talk about it. Then she would have had to reveal everything.

Lizzy unhooked the bike that was hung in the foyer of her apartment and pushed it outside. Then, swinging one long leg over it, she pumped out onto the street and into the night. More than anything right now, she needed to ride.

The cool night air surrounded her, stinging her face and shaking her a little more awake. Lizzy felt the blood pump through her body as she pushed up one of the hills near Allendale. The village scene ahead on 35th Avenue was dark and silent. But then it was well past ten.

Lizzy was alone with her thoughts as she rode on.

Now a new idea entered Lizzy's mind: perhaps Kate was in trouble. Perhaps the odious Mindy Rose found out what happened between them and declared Kate persona non grata, bullied her or worse, fired her. And all because Kate had fraternized with the "enemy."

Lizzy didn't know too much about Mindy Rose, but she did know she was one of the most competitive people on the planet.

As she pumped along, Lizzy convinced herself of what to do next. She would go right home and call Kate, no matter how late it was. After all, she hadn't actually tried calling her. She could feel in her bones that something was wrong.

If Kate needed her, she would come. It was that simple.

With a push up one last hill, Lizzy rode for home, her fingers cold and her face thoroughly chilled.

She had a call to make.

*

Once again Kate rolled onto her back. Blearily, she eyed the clock. It was nearly ten thirty and she was still awake, despite her best intentions.

But then, that's how it was when nothing in your life made sense.

Annoyed, Kate rolled over and hugged her pillow to herself. The voices in her head were all clamoring for attention at once. There was the voice of reason, insisting that nothing she had done was wrong. Mindy wouldn't fire her, even if she did find out she'd been on a date with Lizzy. Instead, she'd pummel her with questions and demand facts, details and information.

Or, knowing Mindy, she'd blackmail Kate into submission by threatening to turn her into ICE if she didn't reveal everything she knew about Driven and its business. That same voice of reason was also quick to remind Kate that she was in no position to quit her job at present. That would be financial suicide, plain and simple.

On the other hand, she could stay with Mindy, no matter how sick she was. It would be like suffering death by a thousand paper cuts. This reality was provided by the ever-cheery voice of doom, which had been playing in Kate's head off and on for as long as she could remember.

The voice of doom quieted somewhat when she'd managed to escape to California. But lately, it had really started to chat her up.

Kate closed her eyes and tried to empty her mind yet again. First, she tried to imagine floating away on a pink cloud. But eventually she gave up on the cloud and moved on to counting imaginary sheep. She was still in the teens when the phone rang.

Kate opened her eyes and grabbed the phone from the table beside her bed.

It was Lizzy.

Sweet Jesus. Now what was she supposed to do?

Reason told her to ignore it. *Turn off the ringer and go back to sleep.* Even if she did pick up the phone, what would she say?

But then there was a small, seldom-heard-from voice Kate couldn't readily identify. Its tone was crystal clear.

Don't. You will only hurt Lizzy if you do, it said.

This stopped Kate cold. She knew why Lizzy was calling. She was calling because, unlike Kate, she didn't have to block her desire and push away her feelings. She was free to call a woman she was falling for, just for the pure pleasure of hearing her voice.

But until Kate was equally free, and able to be honest, she had no business playing with Lizzy's heart.

Sadly, Kate turned off her phone. Then she rolled over and hugged her pillow again. Now she began to cry. It wasn't that being with Lizzy was inherently wrong. The crime would be to lead her on more than she already had.

She had to stand up and make an adult decision. She would either break free, quit her job, let go of her loyalty to Mindy and tell Lizzy the truth. Or, she would live a life that lacked equanimity, forever hiding in the shadows of her own heart.

Kate also understood that the longer she waited to quit, the less likely it was that she actually would. Time had an undeniable way of erasing what once seemed like a good idea. And when she finally did quit, who knew if Lizzy would even still be there?

Kate was profoundly tired of living in fear. The time of reckoning had arrived.

Chapter Fourteen

Mindy Rose came around the corner onto San Pablo Avenue and eyed the Driven sign up ahead. She intended to do a lot more than just cruise by of the garage. Which is all Kate would have done, had she bothered to show up for work.

Kate was playing sick again, or so Mindy assumed. She'd murmured something about nausea and diarrhea, but in seven years, Mindy's assistant had really never been sick. Clearly this was just more of the same lurking subterfuge that had been going on all week.

She slowed down as she approached the garage, where a lunchtime crowd of seven or eight women spilled out onto the sidewalk. Pulling over to an empty spot, Mindy got out of her car and approached the women waiting in line.

One looked up and then another, who nudged the woman standing beside her. They smiled at Mindy. They may have recognized her from the NASCAR races, or her old TV commercials, or maybe from the enormous billboard at the corner of Grand and Broadway trumpeting her garage. "I've got you covered!" said the balloon coming out of Mindy's large, perfectly painted lips.

"Hey, it's Mindy Rose!" someone called.

"Hi, everyone!" she said in a sing-song voice. Moving up and down the line, she began to shake hands and chat with the women, all the while flashing her cosmetically improved smile. Those who didn't recognize her soon caught on that there was a celebrity in their midst.

"That's right, it's Mindy from the Indy!" she called out here and there, just to make sure everyone knew exactly who was gracing them with her presence.

"I've got a little goodie for you girls," she crooned as she worked the line. "But you need to come on over to my place to claim it." Reaching into her pocket, Mindy began handing out small pink coupons that read, 'Good for One FREE Ten-Minute Chair Massage!'

Eager hands snatched up the coupons one by one, and a woman pulled out her phone and started filming the scene. Another woman asked Mindy to autograph her coupon for her. "Hope that doesn't mean you won't use it," Mindy joked, reaching for the ever-present fine-tip purple Sharpie in her purse.

"You must be Mindy Rose," she heard someone say as she was finishing an autograph with a small purple heart.

She glanced up to find a tall, dark-haired butch woman standing in front of her in greasy coveralls. The woman extended a blackened hand, and gave a half-hearted smile. "I'm Lizzy," she said. "Welcome to Driven."

"Oh, hello," Mindy said, declining to shake Lizzy's hand. She turned back to distributing coupons to the women in line. "Here you go!"

"Mindy? Can I speak to you for a moment?" Lizzy continued.

"I'm busy," Mindy replied without looking at her.

Lizzy smiled a slow, reluctant smile. She put her hands in her pockets and cleared her throat. "Just for a moment, Mindy, if you wouldn't mind," she asserted.

Mindy pushed her sunglasses up on her forehead, and turning to Lizzy, drew herself up on her Manolo Blahnik kitten heels and glared at her. "Do you have a problem with me?" she snapped.

"No," said Lizzy. "Not at all. I just—"

"Because you don't own this sidewalk, honey," Mindy continued. "This sidewalk is actually the property of the City of Oakland, and just like you, I'm a taxpaying resident here."

The women waiting in the line in front of Mindy began exchanging looks. The woman filming the scene with her phone moved in a little closer to the action.

"Whoa!" Lizzy said, putting up her hands. "I'm not trying to—"

But Mindy didn't hear her. Instead, she rattled on impulsively. "And for that matter, Lizzy or whatever the hell your name is, you don't own the women's auto garage market either. As if you even could. I mean, look at this place! Look at you!"

"Well, I guess the polite approach isn't going to work here," Lizzy remarked.

Tenika suddenly swept up beside Lizzy. She took Mindy firmly by the forearm and began to hustle her quickly down the sidewalk past the line of waiting customers. Mindy resisted and even tried to pull away initially, but Tenika kept a firm hold, moving with a force she couldn't match.

Mindy found herself following along as if she was no more than a dead leaf caught in the wind. "Hey! Stop it!" she sputtered in protest. "Who the hell are you?" she demanded.

But Tenika pulled Mindy along silently, as if she hadn't heard a word.

When they were about 50 yards from the garage, Tenika finally stopped, but she still had a firm grip on Mindy's arm. She got right in Mindy's face and peered down at her fiercely. She didn't say a word. Meanwhile, Mindy noticed they were alone and felt a sudden, disabling wave of fear.

"Do you know who I am?" Mindy finally managed to squeak.

"I know exactly who you are," Tenika snarled right back at her. "Do you know who the fuck I am?"

Something turned over in Mindy's gut, and she tried to twist away from Tenika's grip. "No, and I don't care. You'd better just let go of me," she tried to threaten. Now Mindy just wanted to get out of there. She looked longingly at her car parked just across the street.

"I'm co-owner of Driven," Tenika hissed, "and if you're in front of our garage trying to flip our customers, you're in the wrong place, girl." Tenika continued to stare Mindy down. "I suggest you get your candy ass out of here and don't even think of coming back. You feel me?"

Mindy swallowed. "I, I…" she stammered.

She tried to pull her arm away but Tenika's grip was like a vice. "Ow! You're hurting me!" she protested.

Tenika continued to stare at her without moving.

"If you don't let me go right now, I'm going to call the police," Mindy snarled.

"You stay on your side of the tracks, Mindy Rose, and you leave our people alone. You understand?" Tenika spat as she released her arm roughly.

Mindy didn't answer. Instead, she quickly retreated across the street to the safety of her gleaming coral metallic I8. Shaking, she jabbed repeatedly at the unlock button until its gullwing door rose up in the air. Then slipping inside, she hit the lock button as the door swung shut. Shifting into reverse, Mindy jerked the car back, then peeled out of there as fast as she could.

She tore past Driven Garage with tires shrieking as Tenika stood there on the sidewalk, arms crossed, watching her go.

In front of the garage, Lizzy was picking up something from the sidewalk. It was the pile of pink coupons Mindy had dropped as she was hurried away.

*

Kate stared at the screen in front of her.

Dear Mindy,

I am writing to inform you of a decision I have made regarding my employment with Mindy's All-Star Garage. For reasons that I cannot get into here

That was as far as Kate had gotten. She stopped and sighed. That was never going to cut it. She deleted the last sentence.

For reasons of my own

No, too vague. Mindy would definitely know something was up. Again, Kate hit delete, and started a new tack.

First, I want to thank you for everything you have done for me.

Really? Exactly what had Mindy done, besides control, manipulate, micromanage and overwork Kate practically to the point of nervous collapse? And yes, she'd helped her stay in the U.S. But at what cost? Kate typed on, aware that sometimes you just had to lie. Especially when dealing with traumatically injured people who were fundamentally unstable.

I truly appreciate the warmth, kindness and support you have shown me.

Kate sighed and reread the phrase a few more times. An emptiness opened up inside her as she looked at the words she had written. Yet again, she was pretending, for the truth was complex. There were times when Mindy had been warm and kind, though mostly that was in the distant past. Still, wasn't it more compassionate to pretend at this point? Just long enough to get out?

Kate hit delete and wiped out the entire letter after 'Dear Mindy.'

How in God's name was she going to actually do this? Maybe she should just arrange a meeting with Mindy and skip the letter altogether. Hell, maybe she should just walk downstairs and quit over dinner. Or right before she did the dishes.

Or maybe she should just flee in the night furtively, like women who escape their abusive husbands. There wasn't one scenario she could imagine that wouldn't have big and painful repercussions.

Lying back on her bed in the sun, Kate stared at the ceiling. She needed to get up and move about. She needed to write the letter. She needed to quit her job. She needed to do *something*.

Kate picked up her phone and stared at it.

What she really wanted to do was to text Lizzy. She wanted to text her and invite her for a walk, so she could pour her heart out to her. Yes, she would quit her job and leave Mindy's house. But until Kate came clean to Lizzy, none of this actually even mattered.

An urgent soundtrack of tension played in her head, the string section building.

Kate typed Lizzy's name into the top of a blank message. And as she did, she could feel anxiety coursing through her body once again. She flushed hot, then cold as she typed on, and her heart beat wildly.

Hi. Are you free to go for a walk with me? I would really like to talk to you.

Hesitating, Kate's finger hovered over the blue arrow. Kate touched the arrow and closed her eyes.

Within a moment came the ping of a reply.

Sure. When?

Kate smiled in spite of herself. It was as if Lizzy had been waiting for her text.

Tonight. Lake Merritt pergola at 6?

The ping came almost immediately.

Fine. Are you okay?

Yeah. Thanks.

Kate held the phone to her chest after typing her reply.

God bless Lizzy. She actually cared. Which is why it was so critical to have this conversation first. Kate simply couldn't stand one more moment of deceiving Lizzy.

Lizzy deserved to know the entire truth, and she needed to know before Mindy could inflict any more damage on Driven.

Then Kate would write her letter to Mindy, or have her meeting, or get out of her job however she could. Mindy would raise hell, of course, but that, too, would pass. And Kate would wind up somewhere. She knew no matter where it was, it had to be better than here.

Lying back against the pillows once again, a weary smile spread across Kate's face.

She would, indeed, get through this.

*

Kate hurried along Lakeshore Avenue past the spice shop, the metaphysical bookstore and the stylish wine bar with its crowd of cocktail hour wine tasters. Kate was now seven minutes late. Hurrying, she picked up her pace to a near run. She couldn't bear the idea of making Lizzy wait for her. Not with the conversation they were about to have.

Kate had been rehearsing what she would say. She'd begin by telling Lizzy how much she appreciated all the kindness she had shown her. And how if it weren't for Lizzy, she wouldn't have gotten through the last week of her life, which had been pure hell.

And then, Kate figured, she'd simply take a deep breath and tell Lizzy the awful truth.

She had no idea how that would go over.

As Kate neared the pergola, she could see Lizzy leaning against one of the columns in the colonnade. She was wearing a dark fleece jacket over her white shirt and jeans, and golden light was playing across her face. She appeared to be studying some ducks that floated by on the lake just in front of the pergola. A small thrill traveled through Kate's body as she neared Lizzy, and she picked up her speed even more.

Sunset was approaching fast and the deep blue sky was fading down to orange along the skyline. A sear of cerise and hot pink splashed the sky behind Oakland's downtown, as walkers and joggers continued on the path along the lakeshore. A lone rower in a scull was making his way down the middle of the lake.

The mood was serene and the air was cool.

Lizzy stood up and waved as she spotted Kate, and Kate smiled. She slowed down to steady herself and she waved back. She approached, slightly out of breath. "Hello," she called. "I'm sorry I'm late."

Lizzy took in the sight of Kate. "It's okay," she said. Then leaning forward, she gave Kate a small kiss on the cheek.

"Hi," Kate replied, still trying to manage the intense adrenaline surge that had just shaken her entire nervous system. Apparently, her heart was trying to beat its way out of her body.

"Walk?" Lizzy asked.

"Oh, yes. Let's," Kate agreed.

They began to walk along the path toward the setting sun, and Kate suddenly found herself struck silent.

"I'm glad you called me," Lizzy said, finally breaking the ice. "I was beginning to worry."

"Yes, I—" Kate began, but Lizzy continued on.

"I mean, I didn't really expect you to call, Kate," Lizzy said. "You said you couldn't date me. Still, a girl's gotta hope, right?"

"Well, that's the thing…" Kate said.

"What?" Lizzy said, with a bemused chuckle. "You mean there's actually hope for us?"

Kate looked down at the path that wound before them. "Oh, Lizzy," she sighed as her prepared speech slipped entirely from her mind.

Kate stopped and took a deep breath. She turned to Lizzy. "I might as well get on with it then," she said. "Lizzy, I need to tell you something."

Lizzy suddenly got a look of intense worry. "What is it?" she said, leaning in. "Are you okay?"

"No! I'm not okay!" Kate blurted. "I'm working for a very damaged person. She's a crook, really, and…" Once again words failed her.

There was a beat of silence. *"And…"* Lizzy encouraged.

Kate studied the concrete path before her, fighting tears, as Lizzy put her hand on her back. "Tell me," she encouraged. "Whatever it is, it will be okay."

"It's not okay," Kate replied miserably, as she closed her eyes. "It's not okay at all." Tears now spilled down her cheeks. "And I am immensely sorry for everything I'm about to say. You have to know that."

"Okay," said Lizzy warily.

Looking up, Kate fixed her gaze on her. "I work for Mindy Rose, and she's trying to destroy your business," she said. "I am so sorry."

"Oh. Well, yeah, I know," Lizzy declared. Then putting her hands in her pockets, she looked over at the lake.

Kate could barely breathe. "Wait—you *knew?*" she stammered.

"Yep," Lizzy replied. Her tone was neither happy or sad. Instead, it was strangely neutral.

"But you never said anything…" Kate's voice trailed off.

"You never replied to my texts, so I guessed you didn't want to hear from me." Lizzy explained. "Though we're still trying to figure out why you helped us."

"I helped you because I wanted to. Because you deserve to succeed. And because Mindy Rose is a monster." A look of deep distress washed over Kate's face. "She is seriously trying to ruin you, Lizzy." she continued. "And I want you to understand, I'm trying to stay out of it. In fact, I'm about to quit. But I just couldn't stand lying to you anymore."

Lizzy paused, still taking in the news. "Well, what can we do?" she finally asked, folding her arms. "At the end of the day, it's probably okay."

"It's not okay. I lied to you!" Kate cried. "I didn't have to lie. I hate lying!"

"But the fact remains that we met, Kate," Lizzy said, hoping to offer comfort. "We found each other. So in the larger scheme of things, this isn't that important, right?"

"Oh, Lizzy," Kate murmured. Then she sighed deeply. "Lizzy, the truth is that I'm undocumented. I'm one of those people that ICE is dying to deport."

The words hung between them like a toxic cloud.

Lizzy was taken aback. She looked at Kate with wide eyes. "Wait a minute—" she said, trying to process the information. "So you never got a green card, or a work visa or whatever people are supposed to get?"

"No," Kate replied miserably. "And Mindy never offered to help me get one, either. I just came on a tourist visa, and I stayed."

"Jesus," said Lizzy, taking it all in. "That is…surprising."

"I certainly don't blame you if you want nothing to do with me now," Kate added. "But you deserve to know the full truth, Lizzy. I'm a very bad bet, indeed."

"Yeah," said Lizzy as she stare in shock. "I see." She nodded. Then she looked at Kate. "Come here," she said with a sigh, opening up her arms. And that is when Kate fell into her warm, deep embrace.

Together they sank onto the cool grass, Lizzy holding Kate and Kate now crying into her shoulder. Shuddering sobs soon overtook her.

They sat there for a long, long time. All around them the oak trees, the vibrant green grass and the tall wildflowers blew in the breeze as evening began, but they didn't move. Lizzy simply held Kate, rocking her and soothing her as she cried and cried.

"I'm getting you all soggy," Kate finally sniffed with a laugh, looking at the soaked fleece covering Lizzy's shoulder.

"Don't worry about it. Here," said Lizzy, producing a clean, but worn red and white bandanna from her pocket.

Kate blew her nose and wiped her face. "I'm so, so sorry about this."

"No more apologies necessary, Kate. I get it. You were caught between a rock and a hard place."

"And I *am* quitting. Tomorrow. I want you to know that."

Lizzy nodded. Then reaching out, she stroked Kate's cheek and pushed her hair back. "Here," she said. "Put your head in my lap."

Gratefully, Kate slid down in the grass and nestled her head into Lizzy's warm, denim-covered lap. "I never want to go back there," she said.

"Okay," Lizzy said as she stroked Kate's cheek. "Don't go back there. Stay with me,"

"Really?" Kate asked as she turned and looked up at Lizzy.

"Yes, I mean, for as long as you can."

Sitting up, Kate looked at Lizzy. "What are you saying?"

"I want us to pick up where we left off," Lizzy said, looking at her evenly. "I mean, if you want to."

"Of course I want to," Kate replied. "But I come with baggage, Lizzy. Serious legal baggage."

Lizzy looked down at the grass and picked a blade between her fingers. "So I'll help you however I can," she said. "And in the end, if I can't…I can't."

That is when Kate leaned over and kissed Lizzy. When their lips touched, it was like a homecoming.

"Come on," Lizzy said, suddenly standing up. She pulled Kate to her feet. "Let's get out of here. We'll go to my house, and I'll make you dinner."

"That sounds completely perfect," Kate said as she stood up, brushing the grass from her skirt. "But, wait, Lizzy." She touched her arm. "Are you sure you're not mad?"

"I'm not mad," Lizzy replied. "I mean, I was pretty damn confused when I figured out you were lying about your job, and then you wouldn't answer my texts. But I figured you had your reasons. Anyway," she shrugged, "I knew you'd be back."

They looked at each other and smiled. Then, once again, they began to walk along the path, fingers intertwined as they went.

"You're also going to be fine, you know," Lizzy said after a long pause.

"How can you be so sure?" Kate asked.

"Oh, I know," assured Lizzy, slipping her arm easily around Kate's waist. "Trust me."

They walked in silence for a minute longer, and Kate's arm circled Lizzy as well.

"This is lovely," said Kate, feeling the first surge of true happiness she'd felt in years.

She truly, deeply adored how this woman rolled. It had been entirely worth the risk.

Chapter Fifteen

"I have no idea how I learned to cook. I guess it was just out of necessity," Lizzy said, dropping handfuls of dried pasta into a pot of boiling water. "My little brother and I were on our own pretty early after Mom died."

"I'm sorry to hear that," Kate said.

Lizzy shrugged and smiled. "I'm tight with my brother. What about your family? Are your parents still gracing the planet?"

"Well, I suppose you could say that," Kate remarked dryly.

"Oh. So you must never see them," Lizzy surmised, stirring the pasta.

"Once in a great while," Kate replied. "They're big drinkers, you know. Da's got a pub. It's difficult."

"Da. That's what you call your father?"

"Yes," Kate replied with an insecure chuckle.

The last hour had been an exercise in grace for Kate. The minute she walked into Lizzy's apartment, with its post-college décor and simple furnishings, she felt completely at home. There was none of the shiny-edged pretense of Mindy's house. No designer fixtures, high-end appliances or Martha Stewart colors here.

Rather, Lizzy had a home with personal touches. It was comfortable, laid back, and easy to move around in. Kate explored while Lizzy cooked. A thousand paperbacks lined the walls of the living room. Houseplants were scattered here and there along with framed black and white prints. There was one in particular Kate noticed, of a country road on a beautiful summer day. The road led to a distant horizon, and the edges of the image were soft. Nature seemed to gleam.

It was something Kate would have in her own apartment.

"I love this," she said to Lizzy.

Lizzy smiled back. "The road to nowhere. Kind of like life, you know?"

Kate moved on to Lizzy's scant collection of cookbooks, lined up before her on a shelf in the kitchen. "Apparently you've used *The Joy of Cooking* a lot," she chuckled. The binding was cracked in two places and the cover was held on with a rubber band.

"Third one I've owned!" Lizzy laughed. "And this one's by Irma Rombauer's grandson. I guess he got rid of the snails and added more quinoa. You know, they even used to tell you how to cook bear meat? Anyway, I started using it when I was eleven."

Lizzy poked at the hissing mixture on the stove—a sauté of onions, garlic, zucchini and sardines, done up simply with olive oil. "It's all about good olive oil...and the Parmesan," explained Lizzy as she gave it a final stir. "Flavors, you know? I really like the Parmigiano-Reggiano they have at Trader Joe's."

Kate wasn't really listening. She was just standing beside Lizzy, smiling at her. Drinking her in.

Kate was here.

Furthermore, she'd told Lizzy the truth and the sky had not fallen, nor had the ceiling collapsed. Her life hadn't disintegrated. Instead, an enticing new pathway had suddenly opened up. Of course, Kate wasn't expecting Lizzy to take her in the minute she quit her job. She didn't expect a thing.

Just the fact that Lizzy hadn't fled, and actually still wanted to date her was huge. To Kate, it was confirmation that she wasn't crazy. And that maybe she really could lasso in some happiness after all. The door to Lizzy's heart remained open. The thought was fairly dizzying.

"Oh, that looks very nice indeed," Kate said, peering over Lizzy's shoulder. "If you're the one cooking I'm sure I will love it."

"Hope so," Lizzy replied. "Taste?" Kate nodded and Lizzy put a steaming bite of sardines and sautéed onion in her mouth. It was nothing less than soul food. "Oh my God," Kate said. "Who knew sardines were so delicious?"

Lizzy laughed. "The cracked red pepper really helps. And here," Lizzy added, pouring a bit more pinot noir into Kate's glass. "You need some of this, too. It all goes together."

Lizzy raised her glass in Kate's direction. "To new beginnings."

"Yes, indeed. To new beginnings," Kate agreed.

Their eyes met and the now accustomed exchange of electricity traveled between them. They both smiled. Then leaning over, Kate kissed Lizzy almost tentatively. But then Lizzy pulled her closer, and began kissing Kate in earnest.

One thing led to another, and their kisses became longer and longer. Before they knew it, they were making their way to the living room couch. They sank down on the cushions together, naturally falling into a comfortable tangle of arms and legs.

"Wait a minute," Lizzy said suddenly, breaking free. She hastened back to turn off the hissing mixture on the stove, pulling it off the burner. "Glad I remembered that," she commented as she hurried back to Kate, who now sat happily on the couch with her feet up on the ottoman.

"Well, you look comfortable," laughed Lizzy, plopping down beside her on the couch. She picked up Kate's left hand and looked at it. "Has there ever been a ring on this finger?" she asked.

"No," said Kate in a small voice. Suddenly, an immense wave of shyness enveloped her.

Sensing her apprehension, Lizzy studied her. "What?" she asked, as she kissed Kate's left hand.

"I've barely even been with anyone since I left Ireland," Kate admitted. "I wanted to, but I couldn't."

Turning toward her, Lizzy brushed back a lock of hair that had strayed across Kate's face. Tenderly, she leaned over and kissed Kate. "It's okay," Lizzy said. "I like that about you."

"Why?" asked Kate.

"Because it confirms something I've thought about you ever since we met," Lizzy explained. "You are the real thing. You're not tough and jaded, and you're not pretentious or fancy, or controlling or manipulative. And you're not one of these women who's on all the time. You're pure. Like some beautiful flower that's about to bloom. You just have to be coaxed out into the sunlight a little."

Kate closed her eyes at Lizzy's words, struck by how they melted right into her heart. She could feel tears coming to her eyes as pure emotion moved through her. This was exactly what she had been wanting for so long, to be with someone who understood her.

Wordlessly, she received more kisses as she felt Lizzy's hand move up her back and caress her body. Lizzy's touch was so sure and strong, Kate literally melted into her arms. It was as if her brain switched off and she simply succumbed. She couldn't stop herself from responding. Now there was no longer any reason to hold back.

Kate leaned back on the couch as Lizzy moved over her and they began to kiss more fervently. Soon she was wrapping her legs around Lizzy as her skirt fell away. Lizzy lowered herself on top of her, and soon her fingers were finding their way inside of her, coaxing her, opening her, bringing her up. Then up just a little more.

There was nothing to do but surrender.

*

They lay side by side, naked on the couch, their various articles of clothing scattered around them—shoes, Kate's skirt, panties,

Lizzy's jeans and Kate's bra. Somehow the two of them never made it to the bedroom.

Kate's head was now cradled on Lizzy's shoulder, and her forehead rested against Lizzy's cheek.

She opened her eyes and looked over at Lizzy, who was gazing at her with an expression of supreme peace. "Hi," said Lizzy with a smile.

"Hi, Lizzy."

"That was unexpected."

"It's what was meant to be," Kate said, pulling herself closer to Lizzy.

"I'm glad you think so, too," Lizzy said. "Are you cold?"

"Mm-hmm," Kate purred.

Rising, Lizzy left for a moment and then returned with a down quilt from her bed. Carefully, she tucked it around Kate, making sure to cover her feet. Kate watched Lizzy move back toward the kitchen in search of something.

Lizzy's naked body looked long and lean as she moved across the room—her legs, back and arms sinewy with muscles not yet grown soft. And she had such capable hands. Such very capable hands. Kate closed her eyes to savor the memory of Lizzy's touch as she made love to her.

"The pasta has to be reheated," Lizzy said, returning to the couch. She handed Kate her wine glass. "But no worries. I guess I pulled it off the stove just in time. Are you hungry?"

"Mmm," was all Kate could manage. She was fairly nonverbal at this point as she savored the aftershocks of sex with the woman she'd been thinking about nonstop for the last five days.

It also happened to be the first time Kate had had sex since leaving Ireland. And it was well worth the wait.

It was what she now knew she deserved.

"I just want to thank you, Lizzy," Kate said as her lover slid in beneath the quilt beside her.

Slipping an arm around her, Lizzy pulled her close. "Oh, it was nothing," she chuckled.

"No, really, I mean it," Kate said as she slid a naked leg over Lizzy's. Her thigh nestled up against Lizzy's vulva, and the pressure felt warm and erotic to Kate. An incredible sense of rightness now passed through her. She felt like her entire life was transforming moment by moment. "Thank you so much," she repeated dreamily.

It was as if her nervous system had finally found a way to relax and let go. The drama of her life disappeared into the background.

"So, Kate," Lizzy began, "are you going to let me help you?"

"Huh?" Kate's eyes flew open. Her reverie interrupted.

"With this situation you're in. With Mindy, and ICE, and all of it." Lizzy looked at Kate with concern. "I have to help you. I mean, I *want* to. After all, you helped us."

"Oh, Lizzy," Kate sighed. She turned to her lover and looked into her waiting gaze. "Thank you for saying that, but Mindy will probably report me to ICE the minute I quit." Kate sighed under the weight of this old, familiar reality. "So I suppose we should just enjoy the time we've got. Be in the moment, as they say."

"Hell, no," Lizzy said, sitting up. "That can't happen." Lizzy hitched the quilt up over her chest and a fierce expression came over her face. It was one Kate hadn't seen before.

"I just found you, for Christ's sake, and I am not letting you go," Lizzy announced. "Mindy Rose can try to get you deported, but she's going to have to deal with me, too," she declared. "And I'm simply not putting up with that shit."

"I mean, there's a million ways to fight this," Lizzy continued. "There are lawyers and safe havens. Oakland is a sanctuary city, so you could hide out if you had to."

"Sanctuary cities are just places where the police don't report you," Kate explained. "If someone else reports you, it does no good. Anyway, I haven't got the money for a lawyer."

Lizzy stared at her. "So Mindy underpaid you as well?"

Kate just looked at her.

"Oh my God," Lizzy whispered. "This just gets worse and worse. Come here," she said, pulling Kate closer in her arms. "We are going to fight this, Kate. There are no two ways about it."

Kate snuggled into Lizzy's arms. She'd never had a defender before. Not once in her entire life. The fact that she had one now seemed precious beyond measure.

Her mouth met Lizzy's and they began the slow waltz back toward lovemaking again. Tongues, arms and legs entwined. Their bodies moved together, dancing now against a backdrop of complete uncertainty.

It was perfect, and it was real.

*

"Just close your eyes and taste," Lizzy counseled.

Kate lifted a steaming forkful of Lizzy's creation to her mouth and slowly tasted the explosion of flavors. There was a note of cracked red pepper, a high key accent to the earthy flavor of the sardines, onions and squash.

"This is utterly amazing," she said, shaking her head. "It's so simple, but I taste so many flavors."

"Can you taste the cheese?" asked Lizzy with a smile. "I love that part."

Kate gazed brightly at her new lover. "You are good at a lot of things, aren't you?" she noted.

"Oh, I don't know about that, Kate," Lizzy chuckled. "I'm good at some things and not others. I mean, I'm terrible at math and forget about balancing a checkbook. And I don't think I've ironed anything since about 1990. Definitely don't open most of the drawers and closets in this place."

"I don't expect perfection," Kate said. "I think you're what I've been looking for, just as you are."

Lizzy blushed a little. "Right back at you. I mean…really, Kate. You are seriously smart. Brilliant, even. You've already saved my business and it's only Tuesday. And," she added with a smile, "now I know one more thing you're very, very good at."

Lizzy kissed Kate lightly, and Kate breathed in happiness. It was bliss kissing Lizzy. Just sitting and eating dinner with her was wonderful. Kate didn't ever want it to end.

"So, listen," Lizzy began, "I want you to stay here."

Of course, Kate had been suspecting this invitation would be forthcoming. From what she could tell, Lizzy never held back.

"That's quite an offer," Kate said. "Why are you so generous?"

"I have to be," said Lizzy. "It's the deal I made with God 10 years ago. Did I tell you about that?"

Kate took another steaming bite of her pasta. "No."

"Oh, okay," Lizzy put her fork down. She collected herself for a brief moment, then turned to Kate. "So 10 years ago, I had a near-death experience. Not a floating above my body, going down a tunnel kind of thing. I mean that I was almost killed."

She gazed at the wall in front of her and continued. "It was the weirdest thing, because I knew something was about to happen when I set off that night." Lizzy paused, recalling the event. "I was coming home from a party. It was 11:30, maybe midnight. And I was coming up 51st Street near Temescal. No one's really out at that time, so biking home was usually safe."

Lizzy paused again and took another sip of wine. "I was pedaling along on the edge of the right lane, and this guy just came out of nowhere going 80 or 90 miles an hour. I remember his car was all black—the windows, the trim, everything. We were the only people on the road, and he clipped me. He didn't exactly side-swipe me, because I noticed him just before he reached me, and I jerked my bike hard to the right just in time."

"I landed with my bike in the middle of a rose bush planted along the sidewalk. I got scraped up. There was mulch in my mouth and a bunch of dirt in my eyes. I got some thorns in my arms, but I was basically okay. I just sat there next to that rose bush for the longest time."

"There wasn't any one around," Lizzy continued. "Not a soul. It was just a moment between me and God."

Lizzy closed her eyes at the memory. "So I say, 'God, what's up?' and she says, 'Lizzy, you're not giving enough.' I mean, she didn't actually say words. It was just a feeling I was getting. But then I got a very clear message, 'Life is a gift, Lizzy. Give it away.'"

Lizzy looked at Kate. "That was it," she repeated. "'Life is a gift. Give it away.'"

Lizzy took another bite of her dinner. "And when I thought about it, I realized I was a majorly self-involved person. I hadn't started Driven yet. I was working for a German dealership making *beaucoup* bucks, tolerating a completely male environment, and feeling basically cut off from everyone. I had no community. I was also drinking too much and screwing around. I was just a mess.

"So that night, I got up, brushed myself off and went home. And I knew I had to put the rest of my life to really good use. There's a 'before' and 'after' in my life, Kate, and that was when everything changed. I knew I had to stop being so freaking self-involved and just get out there and do for others, you know? And that's about when Tenika asked me if I wanted to go in on Driven, so I did that. I eased up on the beers, I started the band and I started working with the kids in East Oakland, teaching them how to fix cars. And well, here we are."

Lizzy smiled at Kate. "Anyway, I figure you're my reward. So I'll be goddamned if someone's going to send you back to the motherland."

Kate smiled at her and lifted her glass. "Here's to generosity," she said.

"But, Kate, you haven't answered my question," Lizzy said. "Are you going to come stay with me after you quit so I can help you?"

Kate swirled the pasta on her fork. She felt overwhelmed at the prospect, but it made perfect sense. She needed help if she was going to survive this next critical step in the process. In fact, she needed Lizzy.

"Maybe temporarily," Kate said, choosing her words carefully. "For a while it would be a godsend. But I really don't want to impose."

"No imposition! None," Lizzy seized her hand. "Kate, I'm asking you to move in with me. Stay as long as you feel comfortable. Stay forever!" she enthused.

"Lizzy—" Kate began as she shrunk away with unease.

"I know, I know, this is total lesbian U-Hauling, but I'm a lesbian, so why shouldn't I? It's honest!"

"Lizzy, I don't—"

"Listen, don't answer now. Go home and think it over," Lizzy said. "See how you feel in the morning. See how it goes after you talk to Mindy. Take as long as you want, Kate."

Kate pushed back her empty plate and looked at Lizzy. Of course the offer was appealing. She already knew she didn't want this evening to end. But Lizzy was right. At the moment, she was in no shape to make any kind of major decision. "I will get back to you about this. Just give me a day or two to quit and get my bearings, alright?"

Lizzy smiled. "Absolutely. Like I said, take your time."

"Thank you," Kate replied, grateful that Lizzy understood. "Now can we go lie down somewhere?" she asked with a sweet smile.

"Of course," Lizzy said. She leaned forward and blew out the candles on the table. Then standing up, she extended her hand. "Come."

And Kate followed Lizzy into her bedroom.

Chapter Sixteen

Kate opened her eyes to the crack of sunlight pouring through the drapes. For a moment, she had no idea where she was. Then looking around, she remembered.

She was in Lizzy's bed. They'd fallen asleep together nearly as soon as their heads hit the pillow.

Now Lizzy was nowhere in sight, but Kate could hear her moving around in the living room. She glanced at the clock. It was just past seven.

Just past seven!

Mindy's furious face blazed into Kate's mind, and she closed her eyes and took a long, shuddering breath. For the previous twelve hours, she'd managed to forget about Mindy entirely. And now she'd have to go home and make up some excuse about where she'd been all night.

But that was okay, because her fury would just organically lead Kate into the next topic of conversation: the fact that she was quitting. And moving out. Even though she still wasn't entirely sure where she would go.

Lizzy now appeared in the doorway. "Good morning," she said as she walked toward the bed with a smile. "I wondered if I should wake you."

Lizzy leaned over Kate and gave her a light kiss. She was fully dressed in clean coveralls and ready for work. All she was missing were her boots as she padded around the apartment barefoot. She stood beside the bed, looking at Kate lying among the sheets.

"Good morning," Kate replied.

"You okay?" Lizzy asked.

"Grand," Kate said sitting up. "And I really have to get out of here. I have to go home and quit."

"Yeah, you seriously do," confirmed Lizzy.

They both laughed. Then leaning over, Lizzy kissed again, pushing her back on the bed.

"Are you going to let me out of here?" Kate asked with a chuckle.

"Oh, I don't know about that," Lizzy joked. "I think this is pretty perfect having you right here. But, yeah," she sighed, finally pulling back with reluctance. "If you've gotta go, you've gotta go."

"I do," Kate said, grinning at Lizzy over her shoulder as she moved toward the bathroom. "But don't worry. I'll be back very soon."

"Oh! Hey," Lizzy reached out to stop Kate. "Happy Valentine's Day."

"It is!" Kate said happily.

"It's February 14th all day long today," Lizzy said, reaching for Kate and kissing her for all she was worth. Her hands caressed Kate's back, coming to rest on her waist. "Best Valentine's Day I can remember so far." Lizzy said dreamily.

"Me, too," Kate gushed. Standing here in Lizzy's arms in the middle of her bedroom, utterly naked, feeling the tough fabric of Lizzy's work clothes, tasting the peppermint of her toothpaste and feeling her pure strength made Kate grow weak again. She just wanted to lie down with Lizzy. She kissed her passionately once more.

"Let's go back to bed," she murmured into Lizzy's cheek.

And Lizzy nuzzled her agreement. But neither of them moved.

"We have to go to work," Kate finally sighed.

"Yeah, but maybe later after work? How about a date?" Lizzy asked. "I mean, we have to celebrate Valentine's Day, right?"

"Absolutely," Kate agreed. "I'll text you. Just let me quit first."

"Tell me how it goes, okay? I'm here if you need anything."

"Right," Kate said as she stepped into the bathroom and closed the door. Lizzy was nothing if not completely supportive, she thought with wonder.

A moment later, she was standing in Lizzy's steaming shower. Hot water poured over her body, rendering her fully awake. Not only did she feel alive, she felt free. And she felt incredibly aroused. Just the memory of Lizzy's last kiss was making this the most erotic shower Kate could remember.

She was alive, all right, and she was immensely grateful.

*

"Well, that didn't take long now, did it?"

Tenika cast an appraising eye over Lizzy as she ambled into the garage. Lizzy was humming an old Doobie Brothers tune, and there was a visible spring in her step.

"Correct me if I'm wrong," Tenika continued, "but I think you got yourself some love last night."

Lizzy just smiled and blushed. "Well, you know." She tried to be coy.

Tenika's joyful cackle filled the garage. "That's what we're talking about, Lizzy. Right there!"

The two women bumped fists. "Okay, okay," said Lizzy modestly. "Let's not wake up the neighborhood."

"Are you kidding? This is big news, girl. You're finally back in the game!" Tenika was enthused. But then she stopped herself. "Oh, but wait. She still working for that psycho uptown bitch?"

"Not for long." Lizzy got a look of bitter resignation on her face. "That woman is really bad news. Worse than we thought. I mean, T, she's evil."

Tenika folded her arms and a dark expression descended across her face as she remembered her sidewalk encounter with Mindy. "Figured as much, but that Mindy chick is not going to be pushing anyone around anymore. Not if I have anything to say about it."

"Hey, T," Lizzy called out. "While we're on the subject, I want to ask you something."

Tenika pressed the button on the lift beside her, and the Toyota she was working on rose up in the air on its yellow metal arms. "I'm listening," she said, and she snapped on some latex gloves. She picked up her socket wrench and ratchet, and ducked under the car.

"I'm trying to figure something out here, so bear with me for a minute, okay?" Lizzy paused and cleared her throat. "What would you think of having Kate join our team?"

Tenika peered out from under the car and looked blankly at Lizzy. "Join the team? Like work here?"

"I think we should invite Kate to come work with us," Lizzy said with more determination.

"And I'm saying I think you're nuts," Tenika said, returning to the brake job above her. She gave the long wrench in her hand a hard twist. "I mean, she's talented and everything. And she obviously knows what she's doing, but Lizzy, just because you're into someone doesn't mean you spend every waking minute with that person. You've got to be sensible here. Anyway, how are we gonna pay her?"

"I *am* being sensible," Lizzy insisted. "Our income has quadrupled just because of *one* of Kate's ideas. Just one! You have to admit that's powerful, right?" Lizzy was selling hard. "Anyway, the fact is that the minute Kate quits, she will be reported to ICE by Mindy."

"Wait a minute. ICE? Like the deportation people?" Tenika asked. She gave a low grown. "So Kate doesn't have a visa or a green card?"

171

"No, nothing," Lizzy admitted. "So basically, this might be the end of a very promising relationship for me."

"Well, *shit.*" Tenika put down her wrench and stared bleakly at Lizzy. "That's...wow." She shook her head.

"You've got that right," Lizzy said. "I don't know what to do, and neither does Kate."

Tenika crossed her arms pensively. "Well, first of all, let's not get ahead of ourselves," she said.

"Kate is quitting right now!" Lizzy exclaimed.

"Jesus," Tenika muttered. She glanced up at the brake job above her. "I'm never gonna get this done," she said. Walking over to the window, Tenika peered out at the scatter of women waiting patiently outside for the garage to open. "We can't solve this problem right now, Lizzy. We've got lube jobs to deliver."

"Yup," Lizzy sighed. "I know."

Her friend patted her on the arm sympathetically as she passed. Then once more, she lowered the Toyota to its spot on the garage floor.

"It will all work out, Lizzy. Just hang in there," Tenika said as she moved toward the bay doors. She inserted the key into the first lock, and the bay door began rising with a rattle.

"How do you know?" Lizzy asked.

"I just know," Tenika replied above the clatter. "Trust me."

Lizzy hoped she was right.

*

Kate opened the back door of Mindy's house gently, not knowing exactly what to expect. Gingerly she peered inside. But the kitchen table was empty, save for a drained coffee cup. Kate picked up the cup, took it to the sink and began to wash it, as if to normalize everything.

She could hear Mindy moving around upstairs. The tread of her feet made the floorboards creak slightly, and each step created just a little more tension in Kate's already churning gut. Now she could hear Mindy walking to the staircase and a slight stab of panic moved through her.

Looking down at the cup in her hands, Kate realized she was shaking. She heard Mindy's voice upstairs.

"Kate?"

"Hi! In here!" Kate called as cheerfully as possible. Mindy did not reply. Instead her footsteps marched down the staircase. Then she appeared in the doorway.

"Where have you been?" Mindy demanded.

"Oh, I was just out doing some things. I couldn't really get back. It was...actually...I ran out of gas, you see, and..." Kate's voice trailed off helplessly. She knew she was flailing badly.

Mindy folded her arms as she looked distastefully at Kate. "You know you're a terrible liar," she said.

Kate swallowed hard. "Oh! Well—"

Mindy held up a warning hand. "Don't even go there," she spat. "Just don't even bother with the lies, Kate, because you're fired."

The word hung in the air. *Fired.*

Kate was stunned into silence. She had no idea how to respond. Turning away, Mindy pushed open the kitchen door. But then she stopped and turned back to her. "But don't worry," Mindy continued. "You can stay here for another week while you sort things out. But we're done, Kate. Don't even bother coming back to work."

Numbly Kate went to her bedroom and sat down stiffly on her bed. She really hadn't counted on this. Not at all. All this time she had incorrectly assumed that the ball was entirely in her court. But it never was.

Only now was reality beginning to dawn.

She'd been meaning to quit as soon as she saw Mindy this morning, but now that urge was soundly gone, diverted by the sheer question of her survival.

It didn't even occur to Kate that she'd gotten exactly what she wanted.

*

Kate lowered herself to her knees, and bowing her head, did something she hadn't done since she was 11 or 12 years old.

She began to pray.

"Jesus, or whoever happens to be listening, first of all I'm massively sorry," she began. But then she stopped herself. Here she was, apologizing yet again, and this time to Jesus of all people, or whatever he was.

Even though she didn't even particularly believe in Jesus, or God, or being a Catholic, she was grasping for spiritual straws, trying to find something, anything, that could save her from her present misery.

"Look, Jesus," Kate began again. "I am really very sorry. I know I've been…"

What? Terrified? Confused? Completely at my wit's end?

This was where religion failed Kate. She was a terrible Catholic because it all made her feel utterly miserable and alone. Slowly, she got back up again and walked to the window. Praying was not going to help.

Jesus, or the angels, or whoever might be out there at this moment was clearly not going to save Kate. She'd have to believe in them, for a start.

Kate watched Mindy's car roll down the driveway. The iron gates slowly opened and the BMW pulled on to Skyline and disappeared.

She could call Lizzy. In fact, she *should* call Lizzy. That would be the right thing to do. Lizzy would certainly want to know what happened. After all, Lizzy was her lover now. Furthermore, Lizzy could help.

Lizzy would also want her to move into her place immediately. And yet Kate couldn't. It was all too much, too soon.

Kate was unable to pull out her phone and make the call. Lizzy's intensity—the very intensity that Kate had been craving only hours earlier—was simply more than she could handle right now.

Yet who did Kate have besides Lizzy? Her entire being had been so wrapped up in Mindy World for the last seven years that she hadn't even bothered to make friends. If she hadn't had a blow-out, she never would have met Lizzy.

Never once had Kate imagined she could be fired. It was as if a cascade of ice-cold water had been thrown over her entire life. Now she had clarity as far as the eye could see, and the picture was frightening.

Mindy had towered over her like some Mad Max dominatrix with sharp teeth and stiletto heels. And Kate was small, beaten and confused, always mired in endless piles of work. ICE always lingered nearby, in their black jackets, waiting to sweep in and deport her.

Kate thought of the videos she'd seen on YouTube of muscular men in their bulletproof vests, shackling their fugitives with chains. Recently the 7-11 across from their garage had been targeted. Kate watched as two unlucky immigrants emerged with their hands up.

That could be me at any moment, she thought.

Somewhere in the distance, of course, was the gleaming beacon of Lizzy. Could she trust that what had happened only a few hours earlier was real? In the midst of all of this chaos, was life trying to hand her a prize? Now Kate was unable to even think about it.

Instead, the wind had been taken out of her sails, and she had been set adrift on a roiling sea. There was no place to go. There was nothing to do. A lawyer couldn't help at this point, if she could even afford one. As an undocumented worker, Kate was without rights of any kind.

Sitting down at her desk, Kate pulled out her laptop and opened up her bank account. She studied the numbers, trying to spin some sort of plan in her head. Yet, she was unable to read the murky balances and transactions that swam before her. It was as if she'd taken some disabling drug, and she couldn't even grip the reality of the black and white figures on the screen.

Kate closed her computer and began to pace around her room. *She'd gotten exactly what she wanted*, she reminded herself. Still her thoughts spun and heaved as she walked in circles. Meanwhile, Mr. Big began to whine and scratch at her door, wanting to be let in. Resignedly, Kate opened the door.

The dog walked in and sat on the rug before her. He looked at her plaintively. "What?" she asked. Mr. Big scratched his ear and lay down.

A text from Lizzy now arrived.

At first, she steadfastly ignored the text, burying her buzzing phone under the pillow next to her on the bed. Finally she gave up and read it.

Thinking of you. **Be strong.**

Lizzy's timing, of course, was perfect.

Now Kate flashed on Lizzy tucking her in beneath the quilt, and Lizzy feeding her a forkful of the amazing pasta. Lizzy looking at her tenderly and pushing a stray lock of hair from her face. And Lizzy's hand on her hip as they spooned together and fell asleep.

Then there was making love with Lizzy. The intensity of her kisses, the smoothness of her skin. The perfection of the muscles at the top of Lizzy's arms. Lizzy's deft, roaming fingers, working her over, filling her. Carrying her to the edge and back, again and again.

It was breathtaking. Yet, the fact remained that if she hadn't fallen asleep in Lizzy's bed, none of this would have happened.

And now, of course, Lizzy was offering the perfect support. And Kate needed help.

Yet, instead of feeling reassured, Kate felt thoroughly disturbed, muddled and jangled. Guilty, even.

If she hadn't fallen asleep in Lizzy's bed, she wouldn't have been fired.

And yet, she'd already decided. Love was what she deserved now, right? And God, or Jesus, or the angels, or whomever was conspiring directly to help her. She could, indeed, trust Lizzy. She could even trust the Universe.

The eternal good girl in her soul could relax. It was actually alright to be fired.

Taking a deep breath, Kate dug her phone out from underneath the pillow once more and did her best to compose a text.

Hi

Hi? That seemed pathetically lame. Really Kate wanted to write 'Help me! I have no idea in hell what to do!' But she couldn't exactly text that now, could she? She couldn't bear for Lizzy to see her so completely torn to shreds. Especially since she'd just been handed exactly what she wanted and needed.

Once again, tears overtook Kate and she lay down on her bed and sobbed for all she was worth.

Finally, she sat up again. Blowing her nose, Kate erased her text and began once more.

Got a shock this morning. Mindy

Kate stopped and erased the words again. She could not even bring herself to type what had happened. How could she explain her current torment? Really, it made no sense.

The phone went back underneath the pillow.

Yet again, Mindy had triumphed in their strange, baseless war. Mindy would always win. And that was precisely why Kate had to leave. For this was where compassion and reality parted company. She had to take care of herself first. That much was now clear.

Rising, Kate stepped into her shoes. "Mr. Big?" she called and immediately, she heard the dogs' toenails scramble down the hallway. He appeared in the door, looking at Kate with excitement.

"Go for a walk?" she asked, and he wagged his tail.

She had to get moving, one foot in front of the other.

It was the only way she would survive.

*

Kate pulled up just beyond Mindy's garage, and hesitated at the edge of the parking lot. She could see a woman getting a chair massage in the window, and beyond that a few shadowy figures at the sushi bar.

What am I doing here, anyway? She didn't want her job back. She honestly didn't.

But how was she going to cope without it?

Stepping on the gas, Kate moved ahead in her lane as a car surged around her, beeping from behind. She'd forgotten to look in her rearview mirror. Trembling, Kate turned right and rounded the corner onto Telegraph. The mid-afternoon sidewalks were busy with people coming and going.

People with jobs, she thought. *Unlike me.*

Kate pulled into a parking spot and sat there, uncertain what to do next. This was pretty much how the entire day had gone. There was enough money to cover a rental for a few months, if she could find one. Even just a rented room somewhere would suffice, she figured.

Once more, she pulled her phone out of her purse and began to cruise the listings on Craigslist. She'd done this twice already today, all the while trying to ignore the unavoidable truth. To reasonably afford housing, she would have to move to San Leandro,

Hayward or Richmond. And if she did that, she would have to commute every day to a job in Oakland.

If she could find one.

Kate tried not to think about the fact that two of these cities were among the most violent in California.

Now Kate surveyed the links under 'Gigs' on Craigslist. *That's what I really need*, she thought. Just something light and temporary. Some kind of freelance job where she could make some fast cash, and no one would stop to think about her legal status.

She tapped on the category heading, 'Creative'. Her eyes scanned the listings. They all seemed to be for things like 'Website Interaction Animator' and 'Spine Artist'. Kate wondered what a spine artist was before she clicked over to Events.

And there was bald reality, staring back at her. 'Sexy Cocktail Waitresses Needed' the first listing said. 'Send pictures.' Someone selling electric bikes was looking for a 'Sales Ambassador,' and so it went, on and on.

Kate closed the app and put her phone away. Could she even do this? Was she able to pull herself together enough to actually go find a job and a new place to live in the next week?

She seriously doubted it. Putting the car in gear, Kate pulled out and headed back toward home.

Chapter Seventeen

Tenika put a squirt of baby oil in her hands and smoothed the oil over her fingers and palms. Picking up a rag, she wiped away the day's accumulation of black grease thoughtfully. Then she began to scrub her nails with a soapy, well-worn brush at the sink.

"What's the problem again?" she asked Lizzy over her shoulder.

"It's not a *problem*, exactly. It's just that I haven't heard anything from her all day," Lizzy replied with a sigh. "I've texted her a few times."

"And?"

"And nothing." Lizzy leaned back in her seat at the cash register and folded her arms. "Something isn't right with Kate, I know it."

"You girls have plans tonight?" Tenika asked, looking up from the sink.

Lizzy shrugged. "We were supposed to go out and do something. I don't know now, though."

Rinsing her hands off, Tenika struck a jocular tone. "Aw, she's just playing it cool. We all do that. Especially if you girls just hopped into bed for the first time. Anyway, maybe she's not into rushing things. Unlike you," she said, lifting her left eyebrow in Lizzy's direction.

Lizzy waved away her partner's ribbing. "Whatever."

"No, not, 'whatever,' Lizzy," Tenika said, looking directly at her. "Seriously. If you want this to work, you've gotta give the girl some space. Even if it is Valentine's Day. And don't forget, some fucking greeting card company made this stupid holiday up. It's not like the Holy See came down and designated it, right?"

"Yeah. I know," Lizzy said sadly. "I just wish I knew what was going on. I mean, she could be in trouble, T."

Tenika picked up her backpack and slung it over her shoulder. "Everything's probably fine. Come on, Lizzy. Just give it a rest."

"Easy for you to say," Lizzy muttered, still disconsolate. "I mean, I'm falling for her."

Tenika smiled at her friend's dilemma. "Then do the right thing," she added gently, giving Lizzy a reassuring pat on the back. "It hasn't even been 24 hours. Give her some space. She'll be back."

Lizzy sighed. "Yeah, okay," she said, still unconvinced. She tried changing the subject. "So what are you girls up to tonight?"

"Absolutely nothing," Tenika said. "Just staying home. A little weed. A little music. One of us will cook...my favorite kind of night."

Lizzy grinned at her partner. "Have a great time. Tell Delilah I said 'hey.'"

They exchanged a hug, then Tenika was gone. Once again, Lizzy was alone with her thoughts.

It was weird, of course. There was no plausible reason Kate hadn't replied to a single one of Lizzy's texts. But perhaps Tenika was right. Maybe she really was worrying too much.

Maybe Kate did just need some space.

Rising slowly, Lizzy picked up her own pack, threw in her water bottle and headed for the door, keys in-hand. Before turning off the lights, her eyes came to rest on the conversation corner.

For a moment, she relished the memory of when they'd kissed, right there on the couch they'd picked out together. How sweet Kate had felt in her arms. She'd trembled a little. She was so perfectly fragile, yet how lovely, open and yielding she had been.

Now Lizzy's mind turned to the simple beauty of making love to Kate the night before.

She thought about touching her body and feeling her respond. She thought about the ease of their conversation, their laughter as they lay beside each other on the pillows and their pure, intimate connection.

Closing her eyes, Lizzy let the memories filter through her consciousness like so much sand between her fingers. Then, snapping off the lights, she let herself out and locked the door of the garage.

It had never been like this before, not ever. Kate might be the one.

She did, indeed, need to do the right thing. Lizzy didn't want to lose what might be a last shot at some kind of abiding love.

*

The silence in Lizzy's apartment was absolute. She slumped on the couch, her guitar abandoned on the floor in front of her. Not even playing music could console her tonight.

It was now 9 p.m., and she'd heard nothing from Kate. Bleakly, it occurred to her that she might not ever again.

Happy Valentine's Day, she thought.

At this moment, it appeared the big love affair was probably not going to happen. And even if it did, Kate was not the person she thought she was.

She hoped Kate wasn't in trouble.

Lizzy's mind had been spinning in the same circle for the last three hours, and she was damn tired of it. Pulling out her phone one more time, she reread her last text to Kate, sent at 4:47 p.m.

Hey, do you still want to grab some dinner tonight?

Clearly, Kate didn't or she would have replied. Unless, of course, the act of quitting her job went far, far worse than she thought it would.

Lizzy's mind played out the possible scenarios. A sick person like Mindy could have given her all kinds of reactions—from cold detachment to rage to possibly physical violence. Lizzy got up and began to pace.

She had to do something. She couldn't just sit around.

Even if Kate was blowing her off, even if she'd had a total change of heart in the last 12 hours—which seemed highly un-likely—it couldn't hurt to reach out to her one final time.

What was the worst that could happen? Kate simply wouldn't respond.

Lizzy pulled out her phone one more time, and contemplated calling Kate. She could practically hear Tenika telling her not to.

But maybe Tenika was wrong.

On the other hand, perhaps something was wrong with Kate's phone? She'd know immediately because the call would go right to voicemail if her phone was off. Hell, Kate's phone might have even been stolen.

Lizzy tried not to imagine Kate lying unconscious in some back alley in Oakland, the contents of her purse now being fenced by some drug addict. Unable to stop herself, Lizzy punched Kate's name on her contact list and her number began to ring. It rang once, then twice, then three times.

Kate's phone was not turned off.

Her voicemail message came on the line after five rings. "Lovely of you to call," began the lilting Irish voice. Lizzy disconnected and threw the phone on the couch. "Shit," she muttered.

Lizzy needed a new plan. Either she did nothing and at-tempted to salvage some last few shreds of dignity by playing it cool and potentially let the most remarkable woman she'd met in years, or maybe ever, slip through her fingers. Or, she kept trying to contact Kate and drove her away.

Fuck it.

Lizzy silenced the never-ending parade of worries in her head and walked over to her desk. Digging into the bottom drawer, she found a box of paper she seldom used. Opening the box, she removed a sheet along with an envelope, and took them into the kitchen. Then picking up a pen, she sat down at the table and set to work.

Dear Kate, she wrote at the top of the page.

This was the letter she'd wanted to write ever since the very first moment they'd met. Back when she thought Kate was an elusive stranger named Marta. Back before she knew the entire story.

Back when she knew innately that something momentous had just happened, something truly life-changing.

Back before she knew she could even feel this way about another person. Before she realized that she did, indeed, believe in fate.

It was time to tell Kate exactly how she felt.

*

An hour later, several balled up, discarded drafts had been tossed into the trash. Lizzy slipped the good letter into the pocket of her fleece. Zipping up her jacket to ward off the chill of a February night, she lowered her bike from the hook on the ceiling. Grabbing her helmet and her light, she took the bike outside to set off for the Oakland hills.

She was going to find Kate's car and leave the letter for her. What she knew was that Kate lived on Skyline Boulevard, not too far from the Chabot Equestrian Center. It was going to be one long hellish climb up Keller, at least an hour biking just to get over to that part of Oakland, and it was beyond pitch black out—on a road with no shoulder, no less. But she'd do it.

Hell, she didn't have anything else to do. And sleep was obviously out of the question.

No, Lizzy was going to do deliver this message the best way she could. And she didn't care if it took all night to find Kate's car. Really, she didn't even have a choice.

It seemed the perfect way to celebrate Valentine's Day.

*

Lizzy wiped at the tears streaming down her face. The night was colder than she'd realized, and the wind stung her eyes as she pedaled with all her strength up the interminable rise of the hill on Keller. It just kept on coming. *The road really should be called Killer,* she thought as she pedaled on.

But soon she reached Skyline, and she'd finally be able to zero in on Kate's car. What she knew about that stretch of the notoriously long and windy Skyline Drive was that there weren't too many houses. So it should be relatively easy to find the car—which, as she understood it, was conveniently parked outside the gates.

Ahead, Lizzy could see a shadowy contour that she hoped was the last of the bloody hill. She'd been slowly cranking along, standing up on her pedals for what seemed like half an hour, and her legs were running out of steam. Breathing hard, she made one aching, final surge for the top of the hill. She pushed herself with everything she had.

Then, finally, Lizzy was at the top where Keller met Skyline.

She stopped and rested for a moment, wiping the sweat from her brow, and she could feel her legs shaking beneath her. She steadied herself, trying to calm her breathing.

A line of old, towering oaks now beckoned her into the darkness of Skyline Drive.

Here, far up in the hills above Oakland, it was like a rolling country road. To her left was a Chabot, a dense 3,300-acre wildland.

Once again, Lizzy started up. When she passed the dark quiet of the equestrian center, she pedaled even faster. There was no shoulder to speak of, and she was alone riding in utter darkness. Yet in the moment, Lizzy felt entirely free. She felt strong and capable, and so very sure of what she was doing.

For the first time all day, she'd managed to calm the worried whirl of her thoughts. In fact, in spite of the cold, her shaking legs and the pain in her lungs, she now felt hope in her fast-beating heart. Lizzy was doing what she did best, acting on instinct and making something happen.

It felt so right to be pedaling as fast as she could on dark, wild roads to deliver her letter.

She had no idea when Kate would see it or how she would react to it, but, in this moment, that was okay.

She was saying her piece because she had to. Letting the chips fall where they may. She knew it was the right thing to do with every fiber of her being.

Lizzy rode on into the inky blackness of the night.

Eventually the tunnel of oaks gave way to a vast, starry blackness on her left. This was the part of Skyline that gave the road its name.

Far down below was the immense tumble of civilization. Layer upon layer of developments, businesses, neighborhoods, nightclubs, churches, tech towers, apartment buildings and ghettos. In the distance was the sparkling water of the Bay. It was always the elegant grace note at the end of the complicated, crowded, random jumble that was the Bay Area.

Eventually, the view disappeared as wilderness yielded, ever so slightly, to suburbia. Only, Lizzy wasn't surrounded by the usual suburban tract homes. The houses that dotted Skyline Boulevard came with acreage, expensive gates and ancient trees. The boulevard now had a large, well-manicured median studded with oaks. It neatly divided the traffic with stately authority.

Lizzy rode on with confidence. She knew Kate's car had to be close by. She knew Mindy Rose refused to let Kate park in her driveway, and given that no other cars were parked along the edges of Skyline, finding it seemed like a slam dunk.

Finally, Lizzy's helmet light picked up a small dark car up ahead. It was, indeed, parked beside a driveway. She slowed the bike and came to a stop. Then Lizzy glanced up the driveway to the large house sequestered behind a heavy iron gate. Her heart began to pound as she got off the bike and approached the car.

She shone her headlamp on the mailbox, and the light revealed a garish race car decorated with the name "Mindy Rose."

She'd found it.

Of course, Lizzy didn't need the mailbox, she'd know the car anywhere. Kate's license plate holder said it all, just as it had the day they met. Lizzy looked at it again and smiled.

Give fearlessly and you shall never want.

The minute she'd seen it, she'd known.

Carefully, she extracted the letter out of her fleece and unfolded it. Pulling back one of the windshield wipers, Lizzy gently tucked her letter underneath it. Then she released the wiper with a soft thud.

She hoped Kate would find it in the morning. And if she didn't, well, at least she tried.

She'd truly done all she could do.

Getting back on her bike, Lizzy contemplated the gate and the house behind it for one more moment. Kate was in there, she imagined. Perhaps she was sleeping. Or perhaps she, too, was wide awake, overcome by the intensity of everything that was happening.

Silently, she sent a blessing in Kate's direction, wishing her well.

Then she was off, her job done. Going back the way she came, Lizzy pedaled fast along the great, winding expanse of Skyline Boulevard, her bike sailing through the cold air.

And as she rode, she gave thanks for the huge, starry universe around her, for sturdy bikes and bright headlamps, for dark, cold nights, and most of all, she gave thanks for Kate.

Whether she ever saw her again or not scarcely mattered in this moment, because now Lizzy understood the truth.

All that really mattered was love.

She was so full of it, she just wanted to give it away.

*

Kate sighed and turned over, trying to ignore the shadowy figures of the packed suitcases beside her bed. When she opened her eyes, she saw them. And when she closed her eyes, she saw them as well.

This is really happening. I'm leaving.

Whether she was ready to go or not, with or without a place to go.

Now turning on to her back, Kate stared at the ceiling, and for the thousandth time that night, she thought of Lizzy. She thought about the night she watched her sing at the garage, her voice so rough and low against her amped up band. She thought about how each song sunk into Lizzy's body as she closed her eyes and wailed.

Her commitment to the music had been absolute that night. Kate smiled as she thought of Lizzy opening her eyes in a sort of post-orgasmic bliss after one of her songs.

She thought about Lizzy cooking, tasting as she stirred, seasoning here and there. And then handing the spoon to Kate, genuinely excited by what she was making. And she thought of Lizzy moving naked toward the kitchen to get their glasses of wine, her beautiful body like an animal in motion. There was Lizzy in her coveralls, checking her tires thoughtfully.

"You okay?" she'd asked after Kate told her about the blowout. It was one of the first things she'd said to her.

Then Kate thought of the way her heart had opened up to Lizzy as they lay together on her couch. Lying beneath her, yielding to her touch, feeling her weight against her own body. She thought of standing in her arms, naked in the morning, and the texture of her rough coveralls against her skin. All of it had been so unstoppable, and so undeniably right.

Now, with a pang of shame, Kate thought about the texts Lizzy had sent, and then the resigned silence that followed when she didn't reply. Lizzy just wanted to help her. But somehow, she felt incapable of accepting help. In fact, now she felt incapable of even talking to Lizzy.

But the last thing she wanted to do was to hurt her.

Kate thought about Lizzy's call that night—the one she tried to answer but couldn't.

What would she even say? *Hi, I lost my job and I need you to save me now, okay?*

The fact was that Lizzy would be thrilled to help. She'd undoubtedly step right up and be the comforting, heroic pair of arms that Kate needed. She'd probably help her solve every last one of her problems. Yet, that was not what Kate needed in this moment, or so she thought.

Kate knew she needed to somehow find her courage again by herself. After years of being browbeaten by Mindy, she needed to stand up and claim her place in the world. But more than anything, Kate felt weak.

She felt as small and terrified as she'd ever felt, and just as powerless. Yet it was nothing less than all-out war now with Mindy. A war that would come to involve ICE, and Driven, and who knew what else if Mindy learned the truth.

Kate knew now that this was a defining life moment for her.

She needed to put Mindy behind her, along with all of the resentment, the trauma, the anxiety, the pain and the relative security of that entire relationship. Then she had to move on swiftly. She needed to find a place to live and a job in short order, and she needed her wits about her.

How on earth am I going to do this? she wondered. Pulling herself into a tight ball, Kate closed her eyes once more, searching for sleep.

She would find her way, one step at a time, she imagined. Just as she had always done.

Chapter Eighteen

Mindy Rose tied on her running shoe with a final tug, and fitted her earbuds into her ears. Then, cranking up "Happy" on Spotify, she headed out the door to the song's opening triad of chords. Its peppy beat carried her down the driveway as she began her morning run.

Jogging in place while the gate slowly slid open, Mindy bopped along to its earnest, upbeat groove. *Pharrell has it right,* she thought. All you had to do was stay relentlessly upbeat and eliminate whatever slowed you down—including people. You really could have anything you wanted.

It had been difficult firing Kate, but it was over. And now, frankly, she didn't give a shit.

Pumping down to Skyline, Mindy turned right and ran past Kate's car. As she did, her eye caught something white stuck to her windshield.

It stopped her.

Curiously, Mindy leaned forward to inspect. It was a letter, the envelope addressed only to 'Kate'. Pulling back the wiper blade, she immediately removed it, and tore the envelope open without hesitation.

Within a moment, Mindy's hands were shaking and an earbud dropped from her ear. Storming up the driveway, she jabbed the code furiously into the gate's security box and waited impatiently for the oh-so-slow gate to make its way open once more. "Come on!" she heard herself snarl.

Then Mindy raced up the hill at top speed to the house as one floppy, forgotten earbud trailed behind her, screaming the climax of "Happy."

She was ready to kill Kate.

*

Kate took a deep breath and contemplated her face in the bathroom mirror. She had fully anticipated her reflection—puffy eyes, red from crying, her hair badly in need of a comb. Gripping the sides of the sink, she lowered her head and took a long breath.

She had to do this. She had to get going.

Turning on the faucet, Kate splashed handfuls of ice-cold water across her face. Again and again she doused herself, and slowly, it began to work. The stinging contrast woke her up, and made her fully alert.

A moment later, Kate toweled off her face and regarded herself once more. She heard the kitchen door slam, then Mindy's feet racing furiously up the stairs. "Kate!" she heard Mindy scream.

Before she could respond, Mindy threw open the bedroom door and waved a letter at her. "What the fuck do you think you're doing?" she screeched as she pushed her way into bathroom.

Kate was still standing at the sink, dumbfounded. "What are you talking about?" she asked as she turned to face Mindy.

"This," Mindy said, waving the letter at her. "*THIS!*" Her face was red, and veins were standing up on her neck. "Read it, you fucking ingrate," she spat, throwing the letter at Kate.

Slowly Kate picked up the letter from the bathroom rug with a shaking hand.

It was a love letter to her from Lizzy.

Somehow, something took hold of Kate as she steadied herself. Folding the letter, Kate looked levelly at Mindy. "What are you going to do, Mindy. Fire me?" she asked coolly.

"You, you…*bitch!*" Mindy erupted, her voice rising. She leaned threateningly toward Kate. "You don't deny it?"

"Why should I?" said Kate, looking right at her. "Lizzy is my lover."

Mindy exploded, her hands waving wildly, fury ripping through her. "YOU'RE SLEEPING WITH THE OWNER OF DRIVEN GARAGE?"

Suddenly, a molten shot of adrenaline mobilized Kate. Now she got right in Mindy's face. "You're goddamn right I am," she hissed. "And she's twice the woman you're ever going to be. She is kind and generous and a great mechanic, and every last woman in Oakland knows it. Especially the lesbians. You're never going to beat her, Mindy. *Never!*"

For a moment, Mindy was shocked into silence. Then she sputtered a reply. "You…you have no idea what you're talking about, you idiot."

"Oh, but I do," Kate continued. "You are a sick, dangerous woman, and I am personally going to make sure that every last media outlet from here to Southeast Asia knows it if you go anywhere near Driven Garage ever again."

Mindy looked at her now, and a shadow of worry crossed her face. For the briefest second, she hesitated. "Go ahead and try," she warned. "And I'll turn you over to ICE."

"Fine," Kate heard herself saying as she closed in on Mindy just a tiny bit more. "The worst they can do is deport me. But you and your so-called image will be ruined for life." Kate paused, letting her words sink in. "I'm sure *People* magazine would love to hear about how you try to run companies out of business, and how you bully your employees relentlessly. I've got some *very* juicy stories that would make some excellent film on *Good Morning America.*"

Mindy's eyes widened. "You wouldn't…" Her voice faltered then she turned away. "Well, obviously you're crazy."

"You're the one who has CTE, Mindy," Kate said as she pushed past her and stepped into the bedroom. "I don't believe Jack Sherman knows any of this...not yet, at least."

Jack was the CEO of The Kiddie Klub, a national chain of pizza restaurants with mini theme parks for which Mindy was still the primary spokesperson. "Too bad," remarked Kate. "They'd probably have to pull all of your commercials. Do you suppose he knows you also hate children?"

"GET OUT OF HERE!" Mindy screamed.

Kate was already collecting her things. Stepping into her shoes, she slung her backpack onto her back, and grabbed the handles of her suitcases.

"No one's ever going to believe you," Mindy insisted. "Jack certainly won't. I'll tell him that you're disgruntled because I fired you."

Kate just laughed. "People aren't as stupid as you think, Mindy. Anyway, I have emails from your neurologist that I'm sure he'd love to see." She pushed past Mindy, through the bedroom door and made her way down the stairs, suitcases in hand.

"*Fuck you!*" she heard Mindy scream behind her. Then there was the sound of glass breaking. She had resorted to throwing things.

Good, thought Kate as she headed out the back door. *Mission accomplished.*

So this is it, she thought to herself as she rolled her suitcases to her car.

This is how she'd set herself free.

*

Kate sat in her parked car looking out at the Bay and holding the letter from Lizzy. She'd waited until she was far away from Mindy and had calmed down sufficiently before she stopped to read it.

She'd sped along Skyline in post-adrenaline rush willing her wild heartbeat to slow as she replayed every last glorious moment of her confrontation with Mindy. There was no going back, ever.

She was done with Mindy, obviously. But she was also done with narcissistic bullies as well, not to mention manipulators. This had been exactly what Kate had needed. It reminded her of an old saying she'd once heard.

God will do for you what you cannot do for yourself.

Perhaps her prayers had actually been answered.

If Mindy turned her into ICE, she would have to leave, of course. But now Kate realized something about herself. She was actually stronger than she'd thought. And she was good at what she did. Her work with Driven, as scant as it was, had proven that to her.

If she had to leave the U.S., she would find her way, and not by pulling pints at the family pub. There was a next right thing. She simply had to determine what that was. And as for where it would be, that, too, would become clear over time.

She could always rebuild. She knew that about herself now.

Kate unfolded the letter in her hands and began to read.

Dear Kate,

I'm writing you because I want you to know I'm thinking about you right now. I guess you probably quit today. I'll bet you're going through something incredibly hard. So here's what I want you to know.

Don't forget that you can do anything you want in this world. You're an amazing woman, Kate. You're talented, you're smart and I believe in you completely. (You are also incredibly beautiful. And did I mention sexy?)

The day I met you I felt that you were special. Then I read what it said on your license plate holder, "Give fearlessly and you shall never want". If you're putting that out in the world, you understand something really important about life. When we give, it all comes back to us, again and again. And you give fearlessly.

Whatever you are going through, don't worry, Kate. I know you're gonna be completely fine.

I hope I get to see you again. I really loved our time together. And even if you decide to move on, please know that I think you are an incredible woman.

I won't forget you.

Lizzy

Re-folding the letter, Kate leaned back against her seat and closed her eyes as a smile spread across her face.
She knew just what to do next.

Chapter Nineteen

Lizzy pulled her bike up at the stoplight and waited, jiggling one foot on the pavement nervously. She thought about her ride up to the hills the night before. And, once more, she wondered if Kate was all right and if she'd gotten her letter.

She reminded herself to expect nothing, and that she was lucky to have what she did in her life. Truth be told, Lizzy was feeling damn vulnerable at the moment.

The light changed and Lizzy set off again, shifting gears to accommodate the small hill ahead. The streets of Berkeley were quiet this morning. A woman came out to pick up her newspaper in her pajamas as Lizzy rode by, and they exchanged a nod. The house was trim and the front yard abundant. Her huge tree loaded with Meyer lemons symbolized all that all was right with life in the Bay.

Someday she wanted that, Lizzy thought to herself. She wanted an actual home instead of an apartment. She wanted a yard to grow things in. And someday, she wanted a wife. She'd realized that during her brief time with Kate.

Really, Lizzy had always assumed she'd never marry. Not just because same-sex marriage had been illegal for so long, but also because she was a romantic loner by nature. More importantly, when she did dive into love, well, her record had not been encouraging.

For Lizzy, love was never easy nor was it particularly stable, either. But then Kate appeared. And Kate did come with some drama, though a great deal of it was not of her own making. She was simply a player who'd fallen into the wrong game. If she could break free and come back to Lizzy, then they might actually have something.

She pedaled on now and thought about the letter she'd left for Kate the night before. In it, Lizzy had begun a conversation about love, responsibility and self-worth. She hoped it was a conversation that never ended. But she also knew that Tenika was right. She had to give Kate space now. She couldn't force things.

Lizzy rounded the corner onto San Pablo and rode along the busy avenue toward the garage. Soon she'd see the beginnings of the crowd that had been showing up for discounted lube jobs every morning. Or at least she hoped she would.

Sure enough, as the garage came into view, she could see a handful of women lined up, some studying their phones and others chatting with each other. It was a convivial, early-morning, coffee-drinking crowd. Business was apparently thriving.

But then a little further up the sidewalk, Lizzy saw something that truly took her breath away.

There was Kate, walking down the sidewalk toward Driven. She hadn't seen Lizzy yet. Instead, she stopped and began to chat with the women waiting in line.

Lizzy pedaled up to the garage and hopped off in front of the women. "Good morning, ladies," she said. "We'll be open in just a minute."

"Lizzy," Kate said, stepping forward.

Lizzy smiled. "Hey," she said softly.

Kate walked over to her, placed her hand on Lizzy's waist and kissed her briefly. They looked at each other. Then Lizzy pulled her in for a long, slow, deep kiss.

The women waiting in line applauded and a few whistled. Kate and Lizzy looked up with embarrassed smiles at first. But then Kate laughed. "Home of the Valentine's Day lube job!" she declared.

"You've got that right!" Lizzy nodded jubilantly. "Hey, everybody! We'll be open in just a sec." She pulled out her keys and taking Kate by the hand, walked her to the door.

"What are you doing today?" she asked.

"No idea. I'm now officially unemployed," Kate replied with a smile.

"Perfect," Lizzy said, motioning her inside.

They stepped into the shadowy garage. Tenika hadn't yet arrived and the place was dark and quiet. "I just want to say I'm sorry for not replying to you yesterday," Kate said, turning to Lizzy. " I had a bit of a meltdown."

Lizzy looked into her face and stroked her cheek. "It's okay," she said.

"I just—"

Lizzy quieted her with another kiss.

"Your letter," Kate began. "It was so perfect. You have no idea how perfect."

Lizzy looked down, a little chagrined. "Well, I'm not much of a writer, but it felt like what I had to say."

"Thank you," Kate said gently. "It was exactly what we both needed."

They looked at each other steadily.

A woman rapped on the glass of the door, and peered inside. Lizzy snapped into motion. "I've got to get to work," she said, unlocking the bay door. "T'll be here soon. We don't have a job for you exactly, but if you're not busy and you want to stay and help for a while, we'd both really appreciate it. But if you have stuff to do, I totally understand."

"I'd love to help," Kate said.

"Well, okay," Lizzy replied. She looked at Kate, her eyes shining. "Let's do this, then."

Lizzy hauled up the bay door, and the women patrons of the Driven Garage began to pour in once again. As they did, Kate and Lizzy smiled at each other, knowing they'd found their way this far.

It was just where they were supposed to be.

About Suzanne Falter

Suzanne Falter is an author, speaker, blogger and podcaster who has published both fiction and non-fiction, as well as essays. Her queer fiction titles include the funny romantic suspense series Transformed. She also writes and speaks about self-care and the transformational healing of crisis, especially in her own life after the death of her daughter Teal. Her non-fiction books include *How Much Joy Can You Stand?*, *Living Your Joy*, and *Surrendering to Joy*. Suzanne's essays have appeared in *O Magazine*, *The New York Times*, *Elephant Journal*, and *Thrive Global* among others. Suzanne is also the host of podcasts The Self-Care Soother and Before the Afterlife. Her free flash fiction can be found at suzannefalterfiction.com, as well as on Facebook, Twitter, YouTube, and Pinterest. She lives with her wife in the San Francisco Bay Area.

Also by Suzanne Falter

Fiction
Oaktown Girls series
Driven
Committed
Destined
Revealed

Transformed series
Transformed: San Francisco
Transformed: Paris
Transformed: POTUS

(All titles by Suzanne Falter & Jack Harvey)

Non-Fiction
The Extremely Busy Woman's Guide to Self-Care
The Joy of Letting Go
Surrendering to Joy
How Much Joy Can You Stand?
Living Your Joy

Made in the USA
Las Vegas, NV
13 December 2020

12887884R00122